Falling Hard

An Instalove Sports Romance

Nichole Rose

CONTENTS

Dedication

This one is for the Weather Girls. It's Raining Men. Hallelujah!

About the Book

He's a mystery she can't wait to solve.

Stella Quinn

Once upon a time, Adrian Kane was a football legend.

He now owns a small newspaper and writes romance novels.

He never leaves his little slice of paradise.

He's a mystery I'm dying to solve.

I'm an annoyance he'd rather forget.

Until I show up at his place during a fierce storm and fall right into his arms.

Now, my job isn't the only thing on the line.

My heart is too.

Adrian Kane

Stella Quinn is relentless in her quest to get me to talk.

She's also a curvy goddess I can't get off my mind.

She wants to share my sad story with the world.

I'd rather forget it ever happened.

Before she turned up on my doorstep, I thought I wanted her to leave.

Now I have to convince her to stay.

My past didn't kill me but losing her will.

And in a town like Spring, Florida, there's *always* another man waiting to step in.

They can't have this one. She's mine.

If you enjoy over-the-top growly men, feisty heroines, and sugary-sweet safe romance, you'll love Adrian and Stella's sweet and steamy story!

CHAPTER ONE
STELLA

"It's ringing," I hiss at Jenna Kirby, my best friend, trying not to panic as Adrian Kane's phone rings in my ear.

"Phones are supposed to ring, Stella," Jenna says through laughter.

I stick my tongue out at her like a three-year-old. She just laughs at me before spinning in another aimless circle in her desk chair. I swear, nothing ever fazes Jenna. I guess that's what happens when your older brother is a former homicide detective. She's always cool and collected.

Me on the other hand? I am *not* feeling particularly cool or collected at the moment.

My heart is pounding, sending adrenaline pumping through my system like I'm in the throes of a major fight-or-flight response. Except there is no danger here. Adrian Kane is safely tucked away in Spring, Florida. And I'm in my office in Nashville. See? Completely safe.

Tell that to the butterflies in my stomach.

Adrian Kane is a Titan. No, not the Greek kind. He played football for the Tennessee Titans. With him leading their defensive line, no one got through. He was merciless, one of the best players in the NFL. Until he woke up one morning and walked away. No explanation. No press conference. Nothing.

That was six years ago.

A year later, he shocked everyone when he published his first romance novel. Now, he's one of the most popular sports romance authors currently writing. He also owns the only newspaper in Spring. *Everyone* has questions about the complete paradigm shift, and everyone from Oprah to Anderson Cooper has tried to get him to talk. He always says no.

I must be a glutton for punishment because when my boss asked for former Titans to profile, I jumped in to suggest Adrian. The man is my hero. While most girls were dreaming about being asked out by the quarterback, I was busy dreaming about playing dirty with Adrian.

Ironic, considering I'm still the same curvy virgin I was back in high school. I'm older, wiser...and as big a mess as ever. For a long time, I thought something was wrong with me and that I couldn't see myself dating anyone because I was somehow defective. At twenty-three, I know better now. The sad fact is, no one ever compares to Adrian.

It's completely crazy, of course. Even I know that. But when I was sixteen, he gave a speech at my school. Some of the football players were being jerks before the assembly started, calling me Stellaphant like they always did because, apparently, being chubby meant I deserved to be compared to an elephant. Adrian overheard them.

No one has *ever* stood up for me like he did that day. He tore into them in front of the entire school, told them they would never be worthy of any woman if they thought treating one like that was acceptable. No one called me Stellaphant after that...and I've had a massive crush on Adrian ever since.

I'm not the only one. Half the female population has crushed on Adrian Kane at some point in the last decade. He's Brazilian-American and is so freaking gorgeous. He's tall and broad, with beautiful golden-brown skin, a wicked smile, and sinful obsidian eyes. Even though he quit playing six years ago, he's still ripped. I know because pictures of him still leak on occasion. He's every bit as beautiful at thirty-three as he was at twenty-three.

It's rare for a man to write romance. It's unheard of for a man to leave a career in the NFL to pursue a career writing steamy romance for women. I am *dying* to know why he made the choice for himself...and not just because my boss may actually fire me if I don't come through.

Don Scarva is a sexist jerk who thinks women should be in the kitchen, making sandwiches and leaving the reporting up to men. Never mind the fact that over half of reporters in the United States are women. Or the fact that I'm half his age and am twice the journalist he is. He made his way to the top by stealing story ideas from other journalists and claiming them as his own.

But that's not my only motivation. I want to unravel the mystery that is Adrian because I might actually combust if I don't know what happened to completely change his life. The man I met at my school that day lived for football. The one who walked away two years later was broken. But even now, his love of the sport shines through. Games come to life in the pages of his novels.

"Hello?"

My stomach quivers as soon as I hear his voice. My memories and my dreams didn't do it justice. It's dark, deadly. Decadent. Like thunder rolling across the sky.

"Hello?" he says again.

"Um, hi," I squeak. Jeez. I sound like a kid instead of a twenty-three-year-old professional. It's a simple phone call. And I cannot mess it up now.

Jenna gives me a big thumbs up from her desk.

I take a deep breath and try again. "Hi, is this Adrian Kane?"

"Depends on who's asking," he growls.

I fight the urge to shiver at his voice. Good grief. He should narrate the audiobooks he writes. I bet everyone would flock to buy them just to hear him read all the dirty parts. I would totally be first in line at that midnight release.

"My name is Stella Quinn. I work for the Nashville Register. I was wondering if you–"

"No."

"No?" I blink, caught off guard by his abrupt denial. "You didn't even give me a chance to tell you what I want!"

"Uh-oh," Jenna says.

"Okay, tell me," Adrian mutters.

"Are you just going to say no again?"

"Probably."

Well, at least he's honest.

"Mr. Kane," I say, refusing to be dissuaded. "My name is Stella Quinn. I work for the Nashville Register."

"You said that part already."

"Would you let me finish?" I huff, exasperated. This is not going at all how I imagined it would go. It's way worse. And I didn't expect it to go great in the first place. I've been trying to reach him all week to no avail. I think he's avoiding me.

Jenna lays her head on her desk as if to hide the fact that she's laughing at me. It's not working. I can see her entire body shaking. My best friend is a savage. She thinks it's hilarious when I get all flustered. She says I get bossy. Which might be true, but still. Where's the loyalty?

"No."

"I'm working on a profile of you for an upcoming feature in our paper—"

"No."

"About former Titans who have gone on to dominate new fields," I say, hoping if I ignore the fact that he's telling me no, he'll stop telling me no. It's not a great plan, but you work with what you've got. And right now...I've got a sinking ship headed nowhere. "I would love to ask you a few questions for the article."

"Stella Quinn."

Holy crap. Does he remember me?

What am I thinking? Of course he doesn't remember me. We met once, almost eight years ago. And we never actually spoke. He just swooped in like Superman to defeat the asshole jocks who made my life a living hell for the majority of my formative years.

"Yes?"

"You called my assistant yesterday."

"Yes."

"And my newspaper the day before."

"Yes?"

"And my publicist."

"She's very nice." I cringe at how defensive I sound. But in my defense...his publicist *is* nice. She gave me his phone number when I explained what I wanted. I think they're related. It took a lot of convincing, but she seemed to like the idea. Apparently, she's the only one. His assistant shot me down cold. No one answered at his newspaper or called me back. And I left, like, five messages!

Rude.

"And you're relentless," he mutters.

"Thank you."

"It wasn't a compliment."

"I'm a journalist. It was definitely a compliment."

He's silent for a long moment, and then the deep sound of his laugh rolls down the line. And wow. He's got a great laugh. My entire body quivers as it washes over me.

"We met once," I blurt out.

Jenna jerks upright, whipping around to face me. Her green eyes are wide with actual panic. "Abort mission," she mouths. "Abort!"

I think it might be too late for that, though. I'm already committed.

"Did we?"

"Yes. Um, you gave a speech at my high school eight years ago." I exhale a sharp breath, spinning my chair to face away from Jenna. She knows the whole story. I made her swear to stop me if I brought it up.

Do I look like I want the ridiculously hot former football star of my dreams to remember me as an overweight sixteen-year-old with a bad haircut and no fashion sense? Hell no. Are you kidding me? But the odds of him remembering our meeting are slim to none, and I'm desperate. Scarva will absolutely fire me if I don't bring him a story.

"You probably wouldn't remember me, but you saved me from the tender mercies of several of my not-awesome classmates," I say before I can talk myself out of it. "I'd really like the opportunity to return the favor."

"What school did you attend?"

"Excuse me?"

"Abort," Jenna hisses from behind me.

I lift a hand and flap it around, silently letting her know I've got this. I definitely don't have this, but she doesn't need to know that. I'll never live it down.

"What school?" Adrian asks.

"It's not important."

"You don't want to tell me?"

"I didn't say that."

He chuckles. "You're a shit liar, Stella Quinn."

"I didn't lie. I avoided the question. It's not the same thing."

"Tell me," he growls.

And lord, I want to give him exactly what he wants.

"Agree to meet with me, and I'll tell you," I say instead.

"You are relentless, aren't you?"

"Journalist, remember?"

He chuckles again. "How, exactly, is letting you interview me returning the favor?"

"If you talk to me, everyone else will leave you alone," I say, hoping I'm not wrong. These things are hit or miss. But if I scoop the story about why he walked away, the mystery is gone. He can go back to writing his sexy stories. I can go back to my dirty fantasies. Scarva's head will explode. Everybody wins.

"Fine."

"What? Seriously? You're going to let me interview you?" I pull the phone away from my face to look at it, just to make sure I'm actually having this conversation and not just imagining it. I'm not.

"You have two days to get here before I change my mind," he growls. "No cameras. No recordings. No talking to anyone else in town about me."

"Two days?"

There I go, squeaking again.

"I need longer than that. I have a boss and a cat and no clean...never mind," I quickly say before I manage to confess that I have no clean underwear. I probably do have clean underwear. But they're in a basket. Which I refuse to fold. The average person spends over two hundred days of their life doing laundry. No one wants to spend two hundred days folding panties. No one.

"Do you want to talk or not?"

"Fine, two days. I'll be there. Thank you, Mr. Ka—"

"What school?"

"Brady High School."

The line goes dead.

I drop my phone onto my desk.

"Holy shit," Jenna whispers.

"Holy shit," I whisper back, staring at her in shock. "Adrian Kane just agreed to an interview."

"You are a freaking badass," Jenna declares, and then her face lights up with glee. "Scarva's going to lose his shit. I'm almost sad I won't be here to see it."

She's leaving for Chattanooga this afternoon to interview Ian Sterling for her profile. He used to play for the Titans too. He's now a billionaire, married to a woman who works with her brother, Jason. It took her all of five minutes to schedule the interview.

"He *is* going to lose it," I whisper. Scarva would love nothing more than to see me fail so he can fire me. He hates me. I think because I turned him down when he hit on me not long after I started. He thought I should be grateful he asked. I may be a big girl, but dating me isn't doing me a favor. Anyone who thinks it is can go fly a kite.

Jenna bobs her head in an excited nod. We both giggle.

I sober quickly. "Crap. I need to book a flight and a hotel and figure out what to do with Gollum while I'm gone and pack." I huff out a breath, not sure what to do with my cat. Gollum is kind of cranky. He doesn't like people or normal cat things. He mostly sits in the window and judges everyone who passes by. Maybe my neighbor, Maya, can watch him for me on short notice. "I can't believe he gave me two days!"

"I wonder if he remembers you?" Jenna asks.

I cringe at the thought, pushing my dark hair back from my face. Puberty was not kind to me. I was teased about my body for so long, I spent my teen years trying to cover it in baggy sweaters and unflattering colors. I hid behind my hair and a big pair of glasses. I've learned to love my curves since those days. Now, I wear whatever I want to wear and don't apologize for it. My hair is still long, but I usually keep it pulled back from my face, and I had laser surgery on my eyes a few years ago.

I'm not the same mousy girl I was back then. I'm still a hot mess, but I'm a more confident mess. That's partially because of Jenna. Like me, she's thick and curvy. We met our freshman year of college and instantly became best friends. She taught me how to dress my curves and hold my head up high.

"I gotta go tell Scarva I won't be in for the rest of the week," I mutter, not looking forward to it.

"You better not even think about letting that troll kill your high," Jenna says, popping her hands onto her wide hips and hitting me with a firm glare. "You just snagged an interview with Adrian Freaking Kane. Scarva should be kissing your ass."

She's not wrong.

"I can't believe he agreed. This is huge!" I kind of want to pinch myself to make sure I'm awake. If this is a dream, I'm going to be so mad when I wake up!

"I can." Jenna's fierce expression softens, a smile overtaking her face. "You're feisty and adorable when you want something. Of course he agreed." She crosses from her cubicle to mine and throws her arms around me in a big hug. "I gotta run, but you better text me updates!"

"I will," I promise, returning her hug. "Love you."

"Love you too."

I stay in my seat and stare into space after she dashes off. The fact that Adrian agreed to talk to me of all people is blowing my mind. I feel a little like doing a happy dance. And a little like calling the whole thing off. Meeting face to face with the man I've been secretly obsessed with my whole adult life is...honestly freaking terrifying.

But I *am* going to write this story. And if he does remember the mousy little sixteen-year-old I used to be? Well, I'll just have to show him that she's all grown up now.

CHAPTER TWO
ADRIAN

"I'm firing you," I growl at my publicist as soon as she answers the phone.

"Again?" Camila asks, completely unfazed.

"Yes." I pace back and forth in front of my desk, restless and irritated. Agreeing to an interview was not on my to-do list for today. I'm not even sure why the fuck I agreed.

Stella Quinn is not like any journalist I've ever met before. I actually like her.

Which is a problem.

Reporters are nosy, invasive irritants. They pry into things that aren't their business and relish spreading what they find to the entire world. I'm a private person with no interest in being fodder for gossip blogs or morning news segments. I've been there, done that. More often than not, the shit they print is true only in their own minds. They've been trying for years to get me to talk, which is precisely why I bought the only newspaper in town. No one here can hound me if I own the damn thing.

I'm still not sure why the hell I invited Stella Quinn to invade my personal space. I think it was that sweet voice. She was clearly flustered which was...cute. So was her bossy little attitude.

I can't remember the last time I thought that about a journalist. Or the last time one got my dick hard enough to pound steel. Actually, I can remember. It's happened exactly once. Today.

Stella thought I wouldn't remember her, but she's wrong. As soon as she gave me the name of her high school, I put the pieces together.

Cristo.

How could I forget?

She's part of the reason I walked away from the NFL.

Her classmates were dicks. It bothered the hell out of me to see her being bullied for her weight. The defeat in her gaze, as if it happened often, pissed me off. She was a beautiful girl, with bright, intelligent eyes and the sweetest smile. She didn't deserve to be treated that way.

Guys like the four who were giving her hell that day are a dime a dozen in the world of professional sports. You give a kid a contract, and he thinks he's special, that he can do whatever he wants with no consequences, regardless of who his actions hurt. That sort of arrogance destroys lives. I know because it destroyed my foster sister's life.

"You must have talked to Stella," Camila says.

"You're on a first-name basis with her?" I stop pacing to glower at the phone.

"We had a nice conversation. She's a sweet girl."

"She's relentless."

"You like her," Camila says, shocked.

"Do not."

"Mmhmm."

"You're definitely fired," I mutter, shaking my head. Camila is impossible, has been since she was a little girl. She does what she wants and makes no apologies for it. I owe her more than I could ever repay. Usually, she keeps people from bugging me. I guess today is not one of those days.

Camila laughs quietly, as unruffled as ever. "You can't fire me. No one else will work for your crabby ass, Adrian. And I'll tell *mamãe*."

"Leave Aunt Áurea out of this."

Camila laughs again. "I'm guessing you agreed to the interview?"

I grunt instead of answering...which seems to be answer enough for her.

"You did agree," she says, clearly surprised. "Wow. I did not see that coming."

"You're the one who gave her my number," I remind her. Considering that my story is her story, too...well, there's a reason she guards access to me as closely as she always has.

My mom immigrated to the United States when she met my father, who ran off with a mistress when I was three. My mother had a good job and a great life by then and opted to remain here instead of returning to her family in Brazil. She died in a car accident when I was fourteen. Her best friend, Áurea Gomes, took me in and raised me right alongside Ana and Camila, her daughters. Ana and I were as close as actual siblings. She gave me shit about being a big football star, I gave her hell for her celebrity crushes. Ana was always shy, gentle. She avoided attention and kept to herself.

Everything changed when I introduced her to Derrick Lovelace, one of my former teammates. Lovelace and I weren't close, but I thought he was a good guy. He certainly acted the part. So when he and Ana hit it off, I encouraged her to give him a shot.

It's a decision I'll regret for the rest of my life.

Ana would still be alive if I hadn't introduced them. She'd have a family of her own, be a nurse like she always dreamed about. Instead, Lovelace manipulated and lied to her, made her question her own instincts. He destroyed her sense of worth, her ability to trust herself, and, ultimately, her life.

She died before she even had a chance to live...and he walked away without facing a single repercussion. I've lived with what he did to her every day since.

Football may be in my blood, but the league is poison. Don't get me wrong, there are good players out there, men who are genuinely good guys doing great things for people. But there are just as many motherfuckers like Lovelace on the field making millions while the organization hides any number of misdeeds for them. Whatever it takes to keep the fans coming back for more.

"You can't avoid talking about it forever, *irmão*," Camila says, her voice soft. "Maybe it's time you told Ana's story instead of letting it eat at you."

"Camila," I warn her.

"I'm just saying, the world isn't the same place it was back then. It's a lot harder for men like him to get away with their misdeeds now. Men like you *make* it harder."

I grunt again, not so sure about that. Lovelace got away with what he did to destroy Ana. The NFL made sure the story never saw the light of day right up until the end. He died two years ago in a boating accident, a hero to a lot of people who never had a clue he was a manipulative, lying piece of shit.

"You do," Camila growls at me. "Do you know how many ex-NFL players go on to become international best-selling romance authors? Or how many donate every penny to women's shelters? One. *You.* You remind women every day that they deserve to be treated with respect and care. Ana would be proud of you, *irmão.* I know I am."

I don't respond, not sure what to say to that. Never once has Aunt Áurea or Camila blamed me for what happened to Ana. They lost a daughter and a sister, but they've stood beside me from the very beginning, treated me like family. Some days, I know I don't deserve that support. Other days, I don't know what I would've done without it.

"Talking to Stella will be good for you," Camila says. "It's time you started living life again instead of hiding away in Florida."

"I'm not hiding."

"When's the last time you left Spring?"

"I leave."

"Liar," she says softly. "You punish yourself for something that wasn't your fault. You didn't know he was a bastard, and you aren't responsible for what happened to

Ana. It's time you realize that too. And you can start by talking to Stella."

"She'll be here in two days," I sigh, giving in to the inevitable.

Camila's shrill scream of joy echoes down the line. I pull the phone away from my ear, cringing.

"You're still a terror," I mutter once she settles down.

"And you love me anyway."

I shake my head and smile. She's right. I do love her. As far as I'm concerned, she's my baby sister. But I'd be lying if I said that's the reason I agreed to talk to Stella. The truth is...she's crossed my mind often over the years, though I've never really been sure why. She'd just pop into mind every once in a while, as if quietly reminding me that girls like her are the reason I decided to write what I do.

After talking to her today, I'm curious as hell about the woman she grew into. The feisty woman on the phone certainly wasn't the same defeated teenager with the bright eyes I defended almost a decade ago. She was fiery, stubborn. Sexy as hell.

My dick hasn't gotten hard for a woman in years. I've been celibate since my first year in the NFL, waiting for...something. Someone, maybe. I don't know. Sleeping around just never interested me much. It never felt right, even before I saw firsthand how badly shit like that can end for people. So I focused on other things, figuring sooner or later, the right one would come along.

And then Ana died, and I moved to Spring, Florida to escape the constant reminders and guilt. Eligible women are in short supply around here. They're outnumbered two to one. Those who do show up tend to be snatched up quickly, claimed by one of the male residents who call this sleepy little beach town home.

"Let me know how it goes," Camila demands.

"Fine. You're still fired."

"Yeah, yeah," she says, laughing. "I love you too."

I shake my head when she hangs up and then toss my phone onto my desk. It lands face up on my keyboard. I've been trying to write all morning and haven't gotten anywhere. Truth is, I don't particularly feel like doing it today.

Instead, I cross to the French doors situated across from my desk and step out onto the back deck. The smell of saltwater calms me. The gentle roar of the ocean as waves crash on the shoreline not even two hundred yards away soothes my restlessness. The sun beats down from over-head, warming the boards beneath my bare feet.

It's supposed to storm like a motherfucker tomorrow, but for today, it's another cloudless, perfect day. There isn't another soul in sight. It's just me, the pale sand, and the roar of the ocean.

Life on the beach has its perks, but it's a lonely way to live.

I've felt that sense of loneliness more and more lately.

Maybe Camila's right. Maybe it is time I stopped punishing myself for something I didn't control and find a way to live again. I'm not convinced talking to Stella is the way to go. I don't want to dredge up the whole sad story and see it turned into gossip and clickbait. Ana was my best friend, my sister. I want to honor her, and the countless women like her.

I didn't set out to write romance. When I started writing, I just wanted to give Ana the happy ending she deserved. But I fell in love with the genre. I'm man enough to admit I want the same things my readers do. Intimacy. Love. Trust. Someone to share it all with. Those aren't female or male desires. Human beings, regardless of gender, crave intimacy and connection. It's simple human nature. We need bonds with others to make sense of the vastness of the world and to find our place in the chaos.

We crave closeness because it keeps us grounded. Otherwise, we're adrift at sea, tossed around like a buoy. I've been treading water for a long damn time, living a half-life because it's what I thought I deserved. More and more lately…it's not enough.

I can't bring Ana back. If God is watching over us, it's up to him to sort out Derrick Lovelace's fate and keep the fires burning. All I can do is learn to live with what happened.

So I'll answer Stella Quinn's questions, no matter how uncomfortable they are. It's about damn time someone heard Ana's story. Fitting that it should be the beautiful, defeated girl who haunts me from time to time.

There's a reason I haven't ever been able to forget her. I just don't know what it is. When she gets here, I intend to find out.

She has questions for me, and I have a few of my own for her.

CHAPTER THREE
STELLA

"Whoa," I whisper, stopping just inside the door to the Munch Box, a diner in Spring. Hot men heaven *does* exist, and I think I just found it. There are gorgeous men everywhere. Including the one behind the counter with his dark head bent as he taps out a text on his phone. I gulp, fighting the urge to fan my face as fifteen curious pairs of eyes focus on me like I'm a whole snack.

"Welcome to the Munch Box," the man behind the counter says, looking up from the phone in his hands. He's smiling, his expression soft. Whoever he's texting must make him very happy. It's plain as day on his face.

I make a beeline for him. The diner is adorable, done up in reds, whites, and light teals that make it feel light and welcoming. Jaunty umbrellas hang over the tables set up on the patio.

"Hi, can you tell me where to find Adrian Kane?" I ask, pasting a bright smile on my face. "I have an appointment with him, but the door to the newspaper is locked, and he's not answering his phone."

"You're looking for Adrian?" The hottie behind the counter—Collin, according to his nametag—says, giving me a skeptical look.

"Yes. He's expecting me."

"He didn't mention anything to me."

"Does he make a habit of telling you his business?"

"On occasion."

Well, crap.

"I have his phone number," I say, hoping that'll convince him.

"He mentioned her this morning," an elderly man seated at the counter mutters, not even looking up from his coffee. "Said she's some journalist from Nashville. She was supposed to be here tomorrow."

"I'm early."

"By twenty-four hours?" Collin asks.

"My plane was fast," I mumble, refusing to admit I hopped on the earliest flight and then drove here straight from the airport. I was worried Adrian would change his mind if I waited. Besides, he didn't tell me exactly when to be here. He just said I had two days. "Do you give all your customers the third degree?"

"Just the ones who come around looking for Adrian," Collin says, then glances at the old man. "You sure this is the one he was expecting, Jenkins?"

"Mmhmm," the old man hums, still not glancing up. "Said she was mouthy."

"I am not mouthy," I gasp.

"You are a little mouthy." Collin cocks his head to the side. "He lives on the beach about fifteen minutes from here. Follow the main road until it dead-ends, then turn right."

"And then what?"

"Drive until you lose the road."

"Are you running me out of town?" I ask, suspicious.

Collin chuckles. "No. His house is at the end of the gravel lane."

"Oh." I give him a sheepish smile. "Thanks."

"Mmhmm." His gaze drifts over my shoulder. "You might want to hurry. The storm is going to hit any minute. You don't want to be caught in it when it does."

"I'll be fine," I promise. It's not even raining yet. "Thank you."

"Welcome," Collin says.

I hurry back out the door, glancing up at the sky. Crap. It's a little after noon, but the sky is already turning dark. Energy crackles in the air too, which is pretty solid evidence that Collin is not wrong about the severity of the storm blowing in. Lightning flashes in the distance, stretching like spiderwebs across the sky. The wind picked up while I was inside, blowing in hot gusts that fling my ponytail into my face.

I quickly brush it out of the way and then head toward my rental car at the curb, my stomach fluttering with nervous excitement. I barely slept last night. I was too anxious about meeting Adrian today. If he dragged me all the way out here just to refuse to answer my questions, I might have to feed him to the sharks. I'm not sure exactly how to accomplish that yet, but I'm pretty good at figuring things out. I'll come up with something.

"Why are there so many hot men here?" I mutter, driving slowly through town. Good grief, there are a lot of them! They're all in a hurry too, rushing about their business in a race to beat the storm. The town itself is charming. Everything is laid out in a big circle, with a gorgeous gazebo in the center. The wind lashes the flowers planted around it, sending them waving back and forth on their stalks.

I drive until the main road dead-ends and then turn right. I did not think Collin was being literal when he said Adrian lives at the end of a gravel lane...but he was. It's barely wide enough to qualify as a road at all. The potholes are bigger than my rental, sending the car bouncing up and down like we're on the ocean as I try to navigate around them.

The bottom of the rental scrapes on those I can't weave around, making me grit my teeth and pray I make it to the other side without leaving important parts behind. There's no way I'm getting my deposit back after this. I should have sprung for an SUV.

Of course the rain starts before I'm halfway down the rickety lane. It doesn't start easy either. One second, it's not raining. The next, it's sheeting down like Jesus opened the floodgates to drown me in a pothole.

"Oh my gosh!" I squeak, slamming on the brakes as the wind sends a branch flying across the roadway in front of me. The hard stop throws me forward in my seat before my seatbelt immediately locks and pushes me backward.

If I get to Adrian's and he isn't there, I'm definitely killing him.

I turn off the radio so I can concentrate and then ease off the brake before creeping forward again, my heart pounding. Driving in the rain is not my favorite thing to do on a good day. This does not qualify as one of those.

"Please don't die, please don't die," I chant, gripping the steering wheel like my life depends on it. I think it might. I can barely see the road in front of me. And it might be my imagination, but I think it's getting narrower. The trees seem to press down on the car from both sides, choking the roadway.

I lean forward in my seat, concentrating hard on the road in front of me. There's not a lot of choice. I certainly can't turn around, and I'd rather not have a tree crush me to death in the middle of nowhere. If Collin lied and this is not the way to Adrian's, I'm going to haunt him for the rest of his life, á la Lucifer in *Supernatural*. I hope he likes Showtunes and country music because I've got a whole lifetime of lyrics stored up and ready to go.

"Oh, thank you, Jesus," I whisper when the trees suddenly end. A beach house looms into view, but it's raining too hard to see much of it. All I can make out is the deck and the white siding. I inch forward, bouncing over another set of potholes that send the car swaying back and forth.

If there's a driveway, I don't see it. And I'm definitely not trying to park in the sand. Instead, I pull as far to the side of the questionable road as possible, my stomach sinking at the thought of hiking the last several yards to the house.

There's no other choice though. I'm not staying out here until the storm ends. It's freaking me out a little bit. I've been through tornado weather. I know the drill. But this is more like Poseidon rose up from the sea in a roar of fury to drown the coast. If Adrian Kane doesn't reveal all his secrets, I'm killing him for sure. Because I have never, ever looked good as a drowned rat...and I didn't bring an umbrella.

I put my phone and car keys into my pocket and shove my purse as far underneath the seat as I can get it. Spring doesn't look like it has a high crime rate, but old habits die hard. I was born and raised in Nashville. Criminals are like the postal service. Neither rain, nor sleet, nor snow stops them for long.

I take a deep breath and then throw the door open. The wind tries to slam it on me before I can wedge myself between it and the latch. I fight my way out, growling at the wind like that's going to stop it. Within seconds, the frigid rain soaks me through.

A loud clap of thunder sends me running for the house, my head tipped down to keep from drowning. Thank God

I wore sensible shoes because trying to navigate gravel and sand in heels would be a nightmare.

I arrive at the deck freezing cold and out of breath. Running is evil.

"Holy crap!" I squeak when a man suddenly looms into view, scaring the crap out of me. And then I get a closer look and come to a dead stop. The Weather Girls were right. Mother Nature was definitely single. Because it is raining men in Spring. And the most perfect one I've ever seen is standing right in front of me. Shirtless. Dripping wet. Hall-e-*lu*-jah.

Adrian Kane is even hotter than I remember. I gape at him, frozen in place. Rain pours down his gorgeous face and slides down his torso. The sweats hanging low on his hips are soaked, clinging to his golden-brown skin. His eyes shoot off sparks aimed right at me.

"Are you insane?" he shouts.

I ignore his question and scrabble up the stairs toward him. Except it's raining and my legs are tired. Naturally, I slip on the last step and plummet toward the wooden boards like a falling star. I squeeze my eyes closed, whimper, and wait for the inevitable crash landing.

Except it doesn't come.

Adrian's arms close around me at the last second, pulling me up against his hard body. Mine immediately heats nine thousand degrees. His breath rasps in his throat, his chest heaving as if he's the one who just ran like a crazy person through whatever fresh hell Poseidon unleashed upon this beach town. He smells incredible, like saltwater, sunshine, and some masculine spice that causes an entire flock of butterflies to erupt into flight in my stomach.

"I should spank your pretty little ass for trying to drive in this weather," he growls in my ear.

And whoa. I am so down for that.

Wait. What?

Before I can process, he scoops me up into his arms like I'm a little kid and stomps toward the door, muttering under his breath about fool women trying to get themselves killed. I assume he's talking about me and mutter, "You're the one who told me I had two days to be here."

It doesn't seem to help his mood any.

Oh, boy. It's going to be a long, long day.

CHAPTER FOUR
ADRIAN

My heart pounds like a jackhammer against my ribcage as I carry Stella inside, the rain lashing us. The crazy woman has a death wish, trying to drive out here in this storm. The road washes out quickly when the creek on the east side of the property overflows its banks. The ground is so saturated that it doesn't take much for that to happen. Fifteen or twenty minutes of good, hard rain is usually enough.

Had the road washed out with her on it, I wouldn't have had a fucking clue if Collin Danes hadn't called to warn me that she was on her way. I was on my way to rescue her when she came racing across the yard like a curvy water Nymph.

Stella Quinn has grown up...in more ways than one.

The feisty woman shivering in my arms definitely isn't the same timid girl I rescued from her classmates when she was a teenager, that's for damn sure. She grew into a certified goddess. She's tall and curvy, thick in all the best ways. Her slacks and pale pink blouse cling to her skin, showing off the curvy body hidden beneath. Water drips from her mahogany hair. Even pulled back in a ponytail, it reaches halfway down her back. Dark smudges of mascara line her almond-shaped hazel eyes. It doesn't detract from how bottomless those eyes appear. She's pink from exertion, twin spots of color blooming in her cheeks.

I've been wrestling with my decision since I got off the phone with Camila yesterday, hesitant to have a reporter in my personal space, prying into my life. I'm suddenly hating the idea a little less.

"You live here?" Stella asks, gaping all around as I carry her into the living room, kicking the door closed behind us.

"Mmhmm," I hum.

"Wow."

I glance around, trying to see what she sees. The cream walls and pale gray furniture give the living room a comfortable, casual appearance. A large flat screen hangs above the fireplace, with a giant abstract painting above the sofa. The blue accent pillows and painting add a pop of color to brighten up the place. The back wall is one giant set of doors that let out onto the back deck, which overlooks the private strip of beach I call my own.

"Put me down," Stella demands, wiggling in my arms.

I ignore her, striding toward the back of the house. I rather like the way she fits in my arms. And she's freezing. It's better for her if I hang onto her for a little while, use my body heat to warm her up again. God knows, I'm burning hot as a furnace with her pressed up against me. She smells like strawberries.

"You need to change," I mutter when she wiggles again. "You'll catch a cold if you don't."

"Cold doesn't cause viruses," she says, matter of fact, her little button nose in the air. She's cute. "It's a myth perpetuated by the fact that cold and flu season aligns with the winter months."

"Tell that to hypothermia."

"Oh, I didn't think about that one." Her bottom lip pokes out for a split second before she smiles brightly again. "But my body temperature is definitely still above ninety-five. I think I'm safe. You can put me down now."

"No."

"No?" She turns wide eyes on me, looking like a baby owl. "You can't just say *no*, Mr. Kane. Bodily autonomy is an actual thing."

"So is being too smart for your own good," I mutter, carrying her into my bedroom. I have a guest room, but since I plan on having her naked and beneath me as soon as humanly possible, I figure we might as well skip the whole pretense and put her where she belongs. "You're cold, wet, and dripping all over my floor. You need to change and warm up."

"I am not too smart for my own good," she mumbles beneath her breath. She doesn't argue when I carry her through the master bedroom and into the en suite bathroom. She gapes again, her full lips parted in a little *o* that makes me want to slide my dick between them just to see how good she looks bobbing up and down on it and moaning my name.

Cristo.

"Your man know you're out here?" I ask...bark, really.

"Why? Are you going to try to murder me and hide my body?"

I gape at her for a minute, not sure if she's serious or not. And then I chuckle. She's a fucking mess in the best way possible. "Depends on how much you piss me off with your questions," I rumble, setting her sexy ass on the vanity. "Might just tie you to the bed for a few weeks to punish you."

"I don't have a..." Her eyes prowl down my body. I see the minute she notices my erection. It's a little hard to miss considering I'm wearing nothing but a pair of soaking wet sweats. The pink of her cheeks deepens to a nice scarlet. She gulps audibly.

"Don't have a what? A man?" I ask, turning to start the shower...and to hide a smile. Judging from the way she's squirming all over the counter, she likes me and my dick.

"Yeah, that."

Then there's nothing stopping me from making her mine. I frown, not so sure her having a man would have stopped me from trying. Not so sure how I feel about that revelation either. It's been a decade since I was with anyone, and I have never pursued someone who was taken. The fact that I might have with this girl is...troubling and not troubling enough at the same damn time.

I'm just not sure what the fuck that means.

"We aren't showering together," she says, her voice a high-pitched squeak. "And I don't consent to you tying me to the bed."

"Ever or just for now? Because it'll be a damn shame if I never get to tie you down, *docinho*." I arch a brow at her, leaning back against the glass shower door to wait for the water to heat. My eyes roam down her body, taking in her hard nipples and the way her skin is pebbled. Not to be cocky, but I don't think the cold is solely responsible for either reaction.

She stares at me for a long minute and then decides to ignore my question with a quick shake of her head. "I can't get in the shower. My bag is still in my car. And there's a hurricane blowing outside."

"It's not a hurricane."

"Are you sure?" She tips her head to the side and squints at me like she thinks I'm full of shit. "It feels like a hurricane. By the way, you live down a dirt road that screams *creepy serial killer*. You should probably do something about that."

"Why? It keeps nosy reporters away. Usually."

"Touché, Mr. Kane. Touché." Her lips twitch in amusement, two little dimples appearing in her cheeks. And fuck me if they aren't the sexiest things I've ever seen. "Seriously, I think your road ate parts of my car. I just hope it's not important parts, or I'm never getting to my hotel."

"Hate to break it to you, dimples, but you aren't going anywhere for a while."

"You plan for our interview to be that long?" she asks, wide-eyed again. "Wow. Scarva's head really is going to explode. I wonder if I can record it for posterity when it happens?"

"The road will be impassable for the next couple of days, Stella. And who the fuck is Scarva?"

"Impassable for days?" Her curiosity turns to horror. "I can't stay here. I have reservations at the Jamison."

"I'll call Jamison and tell him to cancel it," I say before getting back to the important matter. "Who is Scarva, and why is his head exploding a good thing?"

"Jamison owns the Jamison?" She wrinkles her nose at me and then laughs. Her laugh is infectious, contagious. It's not a dainty little sound. It's a full-fledged, irresistible, and unrestrained *laugh*. One I know immediately that she uses often.

The sound washes over me like the notes of a song, sending warmth into places that have been cold for a long damn time. I find myself smiling back at her, my heart suddenly...lighter. It's a foreign feeling. But I like it.

She's fascinating to me. Both because she's beautiful and because she's so full of life. For years, I've wondered what ever became of her. I worried about her. After Ana died, it killed me to think of her struggling the same way because of the heartlessness of others. But grown-up Stella is nothing like Ana. She jumps in with both feet, completely at ease with who she is. She's irrepressible and full of life. Confident.

"I guess you know everyone in town, huh?" she says through her giggles. With the bathroom fogging up from the steam, she really does look like a water Nymph, all soft and rumpled and sexy as hell.

How long do I have to know her before I eat her? I'm sure there's probably a fucking rule somewhere, but whatever it is...I'm also sure I'm going to be breaking it. There's no way she's going to the Jamison tonight or any other night. This town is full of single men. She'll be beating them off with a stick unless she stays out here with me.

"Pretty much. Answer the question, dimples."

"You're supposed to be the one answering my questions, remember?"

"Stella."

"Scarva is my editor," she says, sobering. "He hates me."

"Why?"

"No reason," she says, and then hops down from the vanity. Her gaze shifts from mine, almost casual except for the little flicker of distress in her expression. She's lying. I'm just not sure why. "Um, can I take that shower now?"

I narrow my eyes on her, suspicious. And then she shivers, and I quickly step away from the shower. I'm pretty sure she's right about not being able to catch a cold from the rain, but better not to risk it. Just in case she's wrong.

"Yeah, get warmed up, *docinho*. I'll go grab your bag from your car."

"Oh!" She delves into her pocket, pulling out a set of keys and a phone. She tosses the keys to me. "You'll probably need those. I locked it."

"Smart girl," I murmur, relieved. The crime rate around here is almost non-existent, but one never can be too careful. I don't particularly like the thought of someone breaking into her car while she's here with me. That'd piss me off. "Get a shower and warm up."

"Okay." She gives me a little smile and then waits for me to leave the bathroom.

I pull the door closed behind her, and then stand there like a damn pervert, straining to hear her stripping out of her clothes. Can't help it though. Just thinking about her all naked and wet in my shower has my cock so fucking hard it hurts. I squeeze him through my sweats, trying to get him to stand down.

"He's hot and bossy and shirtless," she mumbles from the other side of the door. "I'm in so much trouble here."

I fight a losing battle trying to contain my smile. My dick isn't going down either.

She isn't the only one in trouble here. I'm sinking like a fucking stone into some level of adoration I've never experienced. It's not nearly as uncomfortable as I thought it would be. For years, she's floated through my mind, haunting it like some ghost whose presence I didn't understand. It's starting to become clear to me.

The protective instinct I felt back then is just as strong today. I always wondered if she was okay and hoped the assholes who tried to break her never succeeded. It's obvious to me now that they didn't. They may have bruised her, but there is no breaking a spirit like hers.

I grab an umbrella out of the hall closet and head out to get her shit, cursing when the wind tries to rip the umbrella from my hands. Water is already starting to pool in the low-lying areas of the front yard. It'll be full by morning.

The potholes on the roadway are full, too, water rushing down the gravel lane in a steady stream. The creek is about half a mile back, just before the last bend in the road. It's probably flowing over the roadway by now too. Once it stops storming, the water will run off relatively quickly. Until then, though, Stella isn't going anywhere. Her little Civic wouldn't make it. Hell, my truck fights to make it some days.

Her being stranded here is looking better by the minute. So long as she's here, I don't have to share her. I can grill her for every little detail about her life, figure out what she likes and whether or not I need to hunt down her boss and have a few words with him. I'm not sure why he dislikes her, but as far as I'm concerned, that tells me all I need to know about the man.

Stella is pure light. Being around her is soothing, peaceful. She's feisty and takes no crap, but she's a little ball of sunshine.

And she packs enough to clothe an entire army.

"How much shit did she bring with her?" I mutter, shaking my head as I try to juggle the umbrella, her carry-on, a duffle bag, the purse I found under the seat, and her laptop bag. Checking all this shit probably cost her a small fortune.

Eventually, I give up trying to juggle it and toss it all in the passenger seat. I slide behind the wheel, grunting when the dashboard digs into my knees. Even after sliding the seat all the way back, I'm crammed into this fucker like I'm in a clown car.

I follow the driveway around to the right and pull up in the carport under the deck. I'm guessing she missed the driveway in the downpour. It's hard to make out on the best days. I'm not a recluse, but people don't come out here often. When I want to socialize, I go into town, or jog down to see Old Man Jenkins, who lives on the beach not far from here. I've always preferred it that way.

Having people in my space irritates me. Unless they're Stella, apparently. Having her in my space is all too appealing.

Once her car is out of the rain, I grab her shit and head back inside to drop her bags outside the bathroom door for her. She's belting out the lyrics to *It's Raining Men*...except she only seems to know the chorus and the verse about Mother Nature being single because that's all she sings of it. Her voice is powerful and somehow sweet at the same damn time.

I walk away, grinning like a crazy person.

She doesn't know it yet, but she is so mine.

"Um, hi," she squeaks half an hour later, peeking her head out into the living room. She's dressed in another pair of slacks, with a flowy white top this time. Her hair is up in a bun, pieces floating freely around her face. Her cheeks are pink, but I'm not sure if that's because she's blushing or if she's wearing makeup. She's got her wet clothes in her arms, clinging to them like they're her only tangible link to the world. "Do you mind if I dry these?"

"Yeah, *docinho*, we can dry them," I murmur, striding forward to take them from her. She hangs on tight for a minute before reluctantly letting me take them.

"No looking at my undergarments," she whisper-hisses.

"No need. I already checked out the ones in your bag," I say, trying to keep a straight face.

"You did not!" she gasps, blanching at me.

I wink at her and head toward the laundry room.

"Adrian Kane! I swear to God, if you aren't kidding..." she shouts behind me.

I chuckle, disappearing around the corner.

"He is completely crazy," she mumbles. "I'm stranded with a crazy man."

"I told Jamison to cancel your reservation," I call, tossing her stuff into the dryer. The clothes hit the metal with a wet plop.

"Thank God someone knows where I am!" she yells back at me.

I chuckle again and push the dryer door closed before starting it. And then I stand there for another minute, trying to will my dick into behaving. I changed from sweats into a pair of jeans to try to hide him, but he's acting like he intends to burst through my zipper like he's the Kool-Aid Man.

What is this girl doing to me? I don't walk around fully erect. I don't laugh and tease and look forward to being stranded with a journalist. Like Camila said yesterday, I'm a cranky bastard most of the time, hiding out in Spring to keep people like Stella from hounding me.

"Your house is beautiful," she says from behind me.

I spin around to find her standing in the doorway, watching me. Her expression is tentative and genuine at the same time, like she means what she said but knows she's not necessarily wanted here. Except...that's not true, is it?

Fuck.

"You hungry?" I growl.

"You don't have to feed me." She grimaces. "Okay, that's not true. You do have to feed me because I'm starving, and I'm stranded on Serial Killer Lane. Oh! I can pay you...or not," she quickly adds when I growl. "This is awkward. Is this awkward?"

"I make you feel awkward?"

"No." She frowns, thinking about it. "But I know you don't necessarily want me here. I guess I feel awkward because you're stuck with me until the storm blows over. No one wants to be stuck with a nosy reporter."

Her explanation makes me feel guilty as hell. She thinks she's an annoyance because I made her think that's how I saw her. That's not true, though. I don't think it's been true since about half a minute into our phone call yesterday. I don't think there's anything this girl could do that would make me view her as anything less than a goddess. Spending time with her is appealing in ways I did not expect.

"Maybe I can cook for you to make it up to you?" she asks, her hazel eyes wide and hopeful. They really are bottomless pools. "I'm pretty handy in the kitchen."

"You want to cook for me?" I ask, surprised.

She shrugs, suddenly shy. "It would make me feel better about invading your space."

"Come on," I say, holding out a hand to her.

She eyes it for a moment before reaching for me. My fingers close around hers. Her hand is soft and warm, small with mine wrapped around it. I marvel at how good that simple bit of contact feels. Touching her is fascinating. My core temperature spikes sharply upward. My dick presses up against my zipper. Energy hums up my arm, crackling like the lightning currently crashing outside. I feel...calm and amped up at the same time, like all the shit that usually bothers me no longer does, and I've been given a shot of adrenaline.

She shivers. I almost ask if she feels it too but stop myself at the last second. Maybe it always feels like this? I don't know. I can't remember ever holding hands with anyone before now. Ironic, considering what I write. But even before being drafted to the NFL, I never dated much or had a real relationship. I spent most of my life focused on football. When that was gone, I turned to writing to fill the void. It's easy to write about intimacy when you crave it so badly.

"You don't have to cook for me," I murmur, pulling her into the kitchen. "I'm...enjoying your company. Besides, I'm the reason you're stranded here. I was a dick yesterday."

"You weren't," she quickly says, shaking her head. "I ambushed you, but you agreed to talk with me anyway. I honestly expected you to tell me to go to hell."

"Why?"

"You never talk to reporters," she says with a shrug. "I figured if you turned down Oprah, there was no way you'd talk to me. Why did you agree, by the way? I'm curious."

"It's about time I talked to someone," I lie.

"Oh."

"You're different than you were in high school."

"You remember me?" She sounds horrified. Looks it too.

"I remember."

"Well, that's humiliating," she mutters under her breath. Her cheeks are scarlet again. "Um, can we pretend you don't remember me?"

"Hell no," I growl.

She pouts at me, though I don't think she even realizes she's doing it. "Fine, but then I'm going to ask you all the questions I want instead of just the ones I need you to answer. And we aren't talking about what happened to my hair back then."

"What was wrong with your hair back then?" I ask.

"Everything!" Her horrified look has me fighting a smile. "It was frizzy and terrible. But we're not talking about it."

"You were a beautiful girl, Stella," I murmur, holding her gaze. "You didn't deserve to be treated the way you were."

"You don't have to lie to me, Mr. Kane," she says, her tone firm. "I know what I looked like back then."

"I'm not lying to you, and stop calling me Mr. Kane," I growl.

She tugs on her arm like she wants me to let her go, except no. "Fine, *Adrian*," she says, emphasizing my name in a way that makes my dick harder. So does the way she rolls her eyes at me. "But I had bad hair, terrible glasses, and the world's worst clothes. It wasn't attractive. I'd rather not talk about it with the ridiculously hot romance author, okay?"

She thinks I'm hot? Fuck yeah.

"You were beautiful then, and you're a goddamn knock-out now, dimples."

She gapes at me for a full minute, her mouth hanging open. I should probably quit while I'm ahead but hearing her talk bad about the girl she was bothers me for a thousand reasons I'm not ready to think about just yet. So I don't stop.

"You saw my dick earlier, baby. You know exactly why he was hard enough to hurt."

"I thought it was an automatic thing," she mumbles.

"Yeah. He automatically gets hard when he's close to you."

"That's...inconvenient. You probably shouldn't wear sweats around women anymore. No offense, but he's hard not to notice when he's ready to sing the national anthem like that." Her entire face turns red. "Please, ignore me."

"I didn't say women, Stella. I said *you*. As in, specifically you." I hook my finger beneath her chin, gently closing her mouth. "And for the record, every time you part those sexy lips, he gets harder."

"Adrian," she whispers.

"Just saying."

"You think I'm beautiful?"

"No, I don't think you're beautiful," I say with a shake of my head, tugging her closer to my body. She's maybe five-eight, but she still looks small next to me. "I *know* you're beautiful." I swallow hard, suddenly nervous for reasons I can't explain. "You've got me thinking about things I shouldn't, Stella."

"Like what?"

"Eating you for lunch," I growl, tipping her head back until her eyes meet mine. "Been thinking about it since I carried you in the house. So unless you're ready for me to do that, I think you need to ask me your questions while I make us food."

"I...I'm a virgin."

"Not helping," I groan, running my nose across her temple, trying to uncover the source of that strawberries and cream scent that's making me crazy. Even though she used my shampoo, I still smell it, as if the delicious scent comes from her and not from some bottle. I inhale her in greedy pulls before I reluctantly back off to give her space. If I don't do it now, I'm not going to do it at all.

And as much as I want to be in her...I don't want to rush this either. I've got about forty-eight hours, tops, to convince her to give me a chance. By the time she's able to leave here, she's going to be mine.

"Go get your laptop, Stella," I murmur, taking another step away from temptation. If I don't, the way she's whimpering is going to make me forget to be a gentleman. "I'll start lunch."

"'Kay," she whispers.

CHAPTER FIVE
STELLA

"Holy crap," I whisper, my hands shaking as I pull my laptop out of my bag. I'm not sure if I died on the way here and went to heaven, or if I'm still in bed, dreaming, but there's no way Adrian Kane is actually attracted to me. It's a statistical improbability. Or impossibility. Whichever one means there's not a chance in hell that a man who looks like him is attracted to a girl like me.

He's a Titan. The Greek kind, this time. Literal freaking perfection. And I'm a hot mess of insecurities and bossiness. I always knew he was hot, but there is so much more to him than that gorgeous exterior. He's grumpy and growly and bossy, but he's also sweet and caring and protective. I didn't expect that, at least not directed at me. Given his feelings about reporters, I was fully prepared for our meeting to be a train wreck from start to finish.

Am I a terrible person for being happy I'm stranded here with him?

"Are you going through my shit?" he yells from the kitchen.

"Yes!" I yell back and then giggle. I actually haven't gone through his stuff...for the most part. I did poke through his cabinets in the bathroom. But only because I needed a hairbrush. And also because I'm a journalist and being nosy is a terrible sickness. I didn't find anything interesting. His cabinets were boring.

His bedroom, on the other hand, is fascinating. A giant set of French doors overlook the deck just like in the living room, and there's a big skylight over his ginormous bed. It's still storming like crazy outside.

The bed is made of some pale wood that somehow looks both rustic and expensive at the same time. The thick comforter is a gorgeous forest green. His Kindle and reading glasses are on his bedside table, along with a stack of papers that I'm guessing is whatever book he's working on at the moment. I really want to peek at it, but I don't.

The rest of the furniture is made from the same pale wood as the bed. A thick green and white distressed rug adorns the hardwood floor, lending warmth to the room. It's pretty without being feminine. It's also ridiculously clean. I think he might be a neat freak because his entire house is freaking spotless.

Small seashells, smooth rocks, and other odds and ends litter the top of his dresser, almost as if he picked them up when he was out on the beach and then forgot them until it was time to empty his pockets. There are a few pictures on top too. One of him and a woman who looks so much like him there's no mistaking the relationship. She has to be his mom. He never talked much about his mom in interviews, but I know she's from Brazil and that she died when he was a teenager. He's maybe thirteen or fourteen in the picture, which would make it right before she died. There are also a couple of pictures of him with two girls and a lady who is a little older. I'm not sure who they are, but the girls look a lot alike. They're all smiling. It's obvious they mean a lot to him.

"Get your sexy ass out here, dimples!" he shouts.

"Hold your horses, bossy!" I yell back, smiling like a lunatic. I quickly grab a notepad and ink pen from my laptop bag, tuck the laptop under my arm, and then head toward the kitchen. There are more photos lining the hallway. When I stop to look at them, I realize they're posters of his book covers. They're very well done, with bright colors and bold fonts. There are a couple I don't recognize.

I memorize the titles so I can look them up later.

"How many books have you written?" I ask when I reach the kitchen.

"Fifteen," he says, not even turning around. He's at the island, putting together sandwiches.

"Fifteen? Wow."

"Are you okay with sandwiches for lunch? I'll cook *empadão* for you tonight," he says. "It's a type of chicken pot pie. My *mamãe* loved it."

"That sounds delicious, Adrian. Thank you."

"Do you read romance?"

"Usually. I've read a few of yours." I've read more than a few of his books, but I'm not telling *him* that I've read every single one I could get my hands on. I drop my stuff on the kitchen table. A quick look out the window convinces me not to plug in my laptop. I don't want the storm to fry it. I'm honestly a little surprised I didn't die in the shower.

"Yeah?"

"You're talented," I murmur. "Why romance?"

"Do you like turkey?"

"Turkey is fine."

"Do you know how much money the romance industry brings in a year?" he asks, turning to look at me over his shoulder. The movement pulls his t-shirt taut over his back. I don't think there's a single place on his body that isn't carved from muscle.

"A lot," I mutter, staring at his ass. My memories and dreams didn't do him justice. He's bigger than I remember, harder. For a long time after he left the NFL, anytime someone was lucky enough to snap a photo, there was this look in his eyes that made my heart ache. There's still a little hint of it in him, but he seems...lighter, maybe. As if whatever weighed on him for so long is no longer quite as heavy.

"Over a billion dollars."

"So you write romance because it sells?"

"No, I write because it's what women want to read," he corrects. "Romance outperforms almost every other genre in terms of sales, audience size, and voracity."

"So picking the genre was a business decision?"

"Partly. Some men in the genre write under female pen-names, but there are only a handful of openly male romance authors out there," he says.

"Why do you think that is?" I ask, grabbing my notebook and pen to jot notes while he talks. I can use some of this for the profile on him. I take a seat at the table, my pen poised and ready to go.

"Romance is considered a women's genre. Do you want mustard?"

"Yes, please."

He shakes the mustard before squirting it onto the bread. "Men shy away because they've been taught to shy away. They're genuinely baffled as to why these books do well, yet they've never actually picked one up to read it. They're more concerned about how they'll look than about what they'll learn."

"Yay, toxic masculinity," I mutter sarcastically.

"Precisely. I'm not interested in upholding an image or belittling the interests of women," he says with a shrug. "That's not the way I was raised, and it's not what I believe. Women are incredible. Romance celebrates them for the goddesses they are, in a way that's inclusive and accepting. I enjoy being able to honor them by telling the stories they want to read."

"Do you feel like you represent the male perspective in your writing?" I ask.

"Partially. There's a bit of a fantasy element to it, in that everything works out perfectly and everyone lives happi-ly-ever-after. That's not always realistic, but it's what we all want for ourselves. It's the future we all hope to find. We all want companionship and intimacy. We all want great sex. Most of us want to find the one person meant for us. Romance allows you to voice those desires in an environment where it's celebrated instead of castigated," he murmurs, carrying two plates and two bottles of water over to the table. "Men want the same things; we're just taught that celebrating those desires makes us weak or inferior. As if wanting love could ever be wrong."

"You're a romantic," I say, smiling.

"I'm just a man who enjoys a happy ending," he says with another shrug before dropping down into the seat beside me. "I like giving people hope and reminding women that there are good men out there, men worthy of them, *docinho*."

"What does that mean?"

"Hmm?"

"*Docinho*," I say, mimicking his intonation. "You called me that before. What does it mean?"

"My sweet or little sweet," he says. "It's Portuguese."

Warmth flows through me. "Your mom was from Brazil. You speak the language?"

"I do." He smiles at some memory. "It was important to her that I speak the language. She taught me a lot about my heritage and about the country she loved. When she passed away, her best friend took guardianship of me. Aunt Áurea taught me what she knew."

"Have you ever visited your family there?"

"I have." He smiles again, almost wistful this time. "It's been a long time."

"Do you catch a lot of flak for what you write?"

"What writer doesn't?" he asks, nudging my plate toward me. "Eat, dimples. I'm not going to stop answering your questions if you take a minute." He waits until I set my pen aside and take a bite of my sandwich before he continues, "It doesn't matter what you write, someone is going to hate it. That's the nature of the beast. Do people talk shit because I went from the NFL to the romance genre? Naturally. Do I give a fuck? No."

I swallow my bite. "You're very blunt."

"Does it bother you?"

"No. I kind of like it."

He grins at me.

"Why did you leave the NFL?"

His grin slips, a shadow passing through his obsidian eyes. "Because it's toxic," he growls, his voice a dark rumble of sound. "When I was drafted, I was naïve. I thought the NFL was a great organization that expected a lot of its players. I was wrong."

"What do you mean?"

"I mean, there are a lot of men wearing jerseys who shouldn't," he says. "The NFL knows this. Far too often, however, unless something hits the news or a player is arrested, the organization and team leadership sweep those misdeeds under the rug, pretend it's not happening. So long as something can be kept quiet, there are no real consequences for bad behavior. To play the game, they expect you to keep your mouth shut about what you know."

"Wow," I murmur, juggling my sandwich in one hand and my pen in the other.

"I went along with it for a while," he says, his voice soft. "And I paid the price."

"What happened?" I ask.

"My foster sister died." His leg bounces up and down, clueing me in to the fact that he's not nearly as calm as he sounds.

I blink, caught off guard.

"Ana was shy," he says, staring out the window. "She didn't date much. But she caught Derrick Lovelace's eye. I thought he was a decent guy, so I encouraged her to give him a chance. I was wrong. He was manipulative and controlling. He cheated on her, lied to her, and made her doubt her own worth and her instincts. Eventually, he broke her."

"I'm so sorry," I whisper, my heart hurting for him. The pain in his eyes is powerful, searing. The same resonates in his voice. I knew he'd lived with a family friend after his mom died, but I didn't know he had a foster sister. It's obvious he cared about her a great deal. I set my sandwich aside and reach out, squeezing his hand.

He doesn't react to my touch. I think he's lost in his story, lightyears away as he shares it with me.

"The day she caught him in bed with another woman, they got into a big argument. He blamed her, said she wasn't enough for him. And then he tossed her out of the house and told her not to come back. She had no clothes, no money. Everything she owned was locked inside with him." Adrian's eyes narrow into little slits, his expression hard. "Ana didn't handle it well. She jumped in her car and took off. When she called me, she was hysterical. It was raining out and dark. I tried to convince her to pull over and let me come get her, but she was inconsolable. She hung up on me...and we never saw her again."

"Adrian," I whisper, stunned.

"She lost control of the vehicle and went off an embankment into the river. It took them two months to find her body." His hand slips from mine. He scrubs both of his down his face as if trying to wipe the memories from his mind. His body is rigid, full of tension, his jaw clenched so hard I'm surprised it doesn't shatter. "She never would have been out there if it weren't for him, yet he never helped look for her. He never showed remorse. He acted like he played no role in her death at all. So did our coach and handlers. They kept the story under wraps, and he suffered no consequences. His reputation was worth more to the Titans and the NFL than her life."

"That's awful."

He jerks his head in a nod. "They decided to let me walk after I got my hands on him. I think they were more worried I would kill him than they were about anything else. I *wanted* to kill him," he whispers, his voice raw. "She never should have been out there that night. She didn't deserve to die like that."

"I'm so sorry," I whisper, reaching up to brush a tear from my cheek. I remember Derrick Lovelace. He was a blond hair, blue-eyed giant with a smile that always looked a little shady to me. When he died, a lot of people mourned him.

My stomach hurts, as if a lead weight sits on top of the organ, pressing down on it. I knew something had precipitated his decision to walk away, but I never expected it to be something so damn tragic. For a long time, people speculated that he walked because he'd done something bad...gotten into trouble or hooked on drugs. I think a lot of people still believe he was allowed to walk to save face over some misdeed.

The truth is so much worse than that. He lost someone important to him, and the man responsible for her being in the car that night suffered no consequences. He was allowed to continue playing the game Adrian loved, his reputation untouched...all while Adrian's was dragged through the mud. And all this time, Adrian never said a word.

"Why didn't you go to the media?" I ask, desperate to understand him. For years, he's been two people to me, the confident man who spoke up for me juxtaposed against the broken player who walked away. Neither was complete in my mind, neither was fully *him*. I've always been so sure of that, but I didn't understand why because I didn't understand him.

He's becoming clearer to me now.

"And tell them what? That Ana spent her last months loving a man who never deserved her? This was before *Me Too*, before society started holding powerful men accountable for their actions. They would have torn her to shreds for no reason other than that they could," he says, pushing his plate away. I don't think he ate more than a bite or two. I didn't either. "Lovelace was a brand to be protected at all costs, someone who brought in millions. In the eyes of the fans and the NFL, she was a nobody. Even dead, people would have placed the blame on her shoulders. I owed it to her and her family to protect her memory."

I'm not sure which is worse: the fact that he's right, or the fact that he knows he's right. We've seen it happen so many times. Powerful men do something terrible, but it's not their reputations that take the hit. People find a way to hold them blameless, simply because it's easier than admitting that we gave favor to someone who didn't deserve it. As a society, we're finally learning a different way, but it's been a lesson fraught with tension and painful, personal reckonings.

"Poor Ana," I whisper, a lump in my throat. "Poor you. All this time, you let people think you retired because you did something wrong."

"I did. I introduced her to that motherfucker."

"You didn't know."

"No, I didn't." He holds my gaze for a long moment, his expression bleak, exhausted. His leg still bounces, his restlessness apparent. He's been living with an albatross around his neck for a long time, keeping his silence to protect the memory of the foster sister he clearly loved. How hard it must have been to endure his pain silently while Derrick Lovelace's face was plastered everywhere. But he did it.

I've had a crush on Adrian for so long, but with his obsidian eyes on me and his truth still echoing in my ears, I fall in love with him. Not with the man I hero-worshipped as a teenager or the gorgeous author whose words make my heart race, but with *him*. The beautiful, brilliant, caring man who carried this secret pain and the hurtful whispers and wildly off-base speculation without complaint.

"You write for women like her," I say as the pieces click into place and my answers materialize in front of me. He's both the confident hero and the broken player, stitched together with trauma and guilt that doesn't belong to him. He didn't go from the football field to the romance genre. He went through hell and fought his way back, trying to do right by his sister the best way he knew how. No one knows Ana's story, but I think he's written little pieces of her into *his* stories, shared her and her hopes and dreams with the world the best way he could: by giving hope to others.

"And for girls like the one you were the first time we met."

I tip my head to the side, not sure what he means.

"I never forgot you, dimples," he murmurs, reaching for my hand. He twists our fingers together. "It bothered me to think that those fuckers were your example of how men behaved. You were just a girl, being targeted by a group of jackasses who weren't taught any better. I didn't get a chance to tell you then that real men don't behave that way. You disappeared before I was finished with them. Seeing the way you were treated changed the way I saw what was happening around me. I didn't want to be the type of man who stood by and did nothing."

"You're not. You're the best type of man," I whisper, my mouth dry.

"Yeah?"

I nod, caught up in his dark gaze. "You were my hero that day," I confess. "No one ever stood up for me like that before. You made me realize that there are good men in the world, and that I didn't deserve to be treated like that. I, um, I kind of crushed on you after that day."

"Yeah?" he says again, his voice low, gritty. He lets go of my fingers, wrapping his big hand around my wrist. Sparks jump from his skin to mine, sending warmth crawling up my arm. "You compared other men to me, *docinho*?"

I bob my head in a nod.

"No one ever measured up, did they?" He slides his hand higher, his rough palm abrading my skin in a way that has heat pooling in my belly and moisture trickling between my thighs.

"I..." I shake my head.

"That's because your heart knew what I'm just realizing, baby."

"W...what?"

"That you're mine," he growls, heat flaring in his eyes. It rushes over me in a wave, igniting me from the inside out. Those parts of me that have only ever craved him light up like a solar flare streaking across the sky.

I think he might be right. Actually, I know he is. I was meant to be his.

"I'm going to kiss you now, Stella. Stop me."

"Don't stop," I whisper instead, aching to feel his lips on mine. To know if he tastes as good as I've always imagined, if he feels as good as I always dreamed.

He wraps his hand around the back of my neck, gently applying pressure until I lean forward, meeting him halfway. His breath whispers across my lips. And then his lips touch mine. For someone so big, he's soft, careful. For a long moment, he simply brushes his lips against mine in sweet passes that have my entire body quivering.

"Adrian," I whimper.

"There it is," he growls. Gentleness dies. He yanks me forward, practically dragging me into his lap as his kiss grows deeper, hotter. I barely have time to wrap my legs around him before he claims my mouth exactly as if it belongs to him, growling as he does it. His hands dig into my hips, holding me still.

I feel his erection against my center, hard and insistent. The entire world spirals away, leaving just the two of us.

I kiss him back eagerly. I'm not real sure what I'm doing, but he seems to like it when I mimic what he does. His grip grows more possessive, his growls louder.

I run my hands all over his shoulders and back, trying to feel as much of him as possible. His body is a furnace, searing me with heat and desire in equal measure. There isn't a soft spot on him. He's a Titan in every sense of the word.

He shifts beneath me, and his erection bumps against my clit.

"Oh," I moan, my head lolling on my shoulders as pure bliss rips through me.

"Fuck," he growls, biting my lip.

I dig my nails into his shoulders and wiggle, chasing the same feeling that just shot through me like an arrow. He bites my lip again, using his hands to rock my hips into his. I've touched myself before, gotten myself off. But it did not feel remotely close to this good.

"Adrian," I moan, writhing on top of him.

His teeth close around my right nipple, and my moan turns to a keening cry. My entire body trembles in response, my core clenching hard as I feel that sharp bite everywhere. I never imagined pain could feel so damn good.

"I can't wait until you're wet and naked in my bed," he growls, pulling the top of my blouse down to expose my cleavage. He kisses all over it as if he can't stop himself. "I'm going to wreck this gorgeous little body, Stella."

"Adrian," I whimper, liking the sound of that.

"Come for me before I tumble you to the floor and fuck you right here," he demands. He rocks me against him again, using his grip on my ass to grind me against his erection. It strikes against my clit with startling accuracy, sending me spiraling toward an orgasm that's almost overwhelmingly large.

I chase the pleasure it promises, shameless and greedy. Every part of my body aches, demanding release. He seems to know it too. He kisses all over my chest, muttering the dirty things I've only read in books. I didn't even know men actually said those things, but they roll from his sinful lips without hesitation. He doesn't hide what he wants to do to me or how I'm making him feel. He tells me baldly, his voice like gravel.

"Been thinking about playing with these tits since you fell into my arms," he mutters, sucking me through my shirt. "I want to know how good they look covered in my cum, *docinho*. You're going to let me do it too, aren't you?"

"Yes," I gasp, trembling at the thought.

"Good." He releases his grip on my ass, only to smack it. "I'm going to be coming on this round ass soon too. You'll be covered in sweat and cum and love every minute of it, dirty little girl."

I think he's right because nothing he's said so far sounds like a bad idea to me. In fact, it all sounds like heaven. I've been hanging onto my virginity for years, saving it...for him, I'm honest enough to admit to myself. I wanted him to be the one to claim it. Even before I knew what that meant, I wanted it. From the day I first set eyes on him, I think I knew it was meant to be his.

That's why I've obsessed about him for so long. That's why no one else measured up. Even if my mind didn't consciously know I was supposed to be his, my heart and my body knew. That's why I never could forget him or see beyond him. He was too big, too bright, too *there*. He's always been right there, hovering like a specter, silently waiting for me to grow up and come to him.

I'm all grown up, and I'm here now.

"Come for me, Stella," he growls and then smacks my ass again. "Let me see it."

My body responds as if it's his to command. My core clenches, my inner muscles spasming as if trying to find something to cling onto. I dig my nails into his shoulder and grind down on him again. My orgasm slams into me, hitting like a tidal wave.

I cry out his name, writhing through it as bright colors explode behind my lids, striking harder than the lightning still flashing in the sky outside. It seems to go on forever, endless waves of ecstasy churning through me. Adrian holds me close, running his hands and mouth all over me as pure bliss replaces the blood in my veins.

By the time I slump against him, I'm sweaty and out of breath. My entire body is overly sensitive, my heart pounding so hard it reminds me of one of those old cartoons where it beats out of their chests. I think he just ruined me...and I think I'm perfectly okay with that.

"Best interview ever," I mumble, pressing my face to his throat.

His soft laugh hits me right in the heart.

Chapter Six
ADRIAN

"Why did you move to Spring?" Stella asks, peeking at me out of the corner of her eye after dinner. We're on the couch, her laptop forgotten on the coffee table. She's supposed to be working. Instead, she's watching me pretend I'm not watching her instead of the movie playing on the television.

I can't keep my eyes off her. She's so damn beautiful. There's an artlessness about her, an innocence I find myself wanting to protect. Somehow, despite everything her classmates put her through, she's still full of love and hope. She's bright and loud and makes no apologies for who she is. I think I needed to see that, more than I realized.

Stella isn't Ana. She's a survivor, a fighter. She came out the other side of what she went through unbroken, stronger. Knowing I had some part in helping her, that I showed her that there are good men in this world...I needed that.

It's still storming, thank God. I'm not ready to let her go just yet.

Sharing Ana's story with her helped in ways I didn't expect.

She's been asking me questions on and off all day. When she's not asking me about every detail of my life, I've been quizzing her on hers. Everything she reveals feels a little like déjà vu, as if I knew it—or knew her—on a subconscious level and merely forgot the details.

"I have a buddy here," I murmur in response to her question. "Got tired of being hounded by reporters and paparazzi, so I crashed with him for a while after I left the NFL. The place grew on me. I like being close to the water."

"Oh." She mulls that over. "Why are there so many hot men here?"

I narrow my eyes on her, possessiveness roiling through me in a cloud.

"I'm serious," she says, laughing at my expression. "It's like hot men heaven in this town. That's not normal, Adrian. Why are there so many more men than women here?"

"The town does have more men than women," I agree with a shrug. Everyone here knows it. Everyone has a theory as to why that might be the case. But I've never really cared one way or another. "No one really knows why. It just happened that way, I guess."

"It's an anomaly. Economic divides usually trend the other way, with more women inhabiting big cities than men. I've never seen it play out the opposite way, especially in a town this size."

"Single women don't last long around here."

"Really?"

"I've printed half a dozen engagement announcements in the last few weeks. And that's not even half of them," I say.

"Wow."

I smile when I see the little furrow in her brow. She's dying to know what makes this town different, or what makes the people here different. I can see it in her eyes. "You're curious about everything, aren't you?"

"Journalist, remember?"

"Why journalism?"

"Because I'm curious about everything."

"Smart ass."

She laughs. "I like knowing things. Journalism seemed like a fun way to sate my curiosity and tell the stories people want to hear. I like what I do most of the time."

"Only most of the time?"

"My editor is the devil."

"Scarva? Why don't you like him?" I ask, curious. This is the second time she's mentioned him in a negative way. I don't like it. There isn't a petty or mean bone in her body. If she doesn't like him, there's a reason for it.

"Because he's the devil," she huffs, fidgeting.

"Why, Stella? Tell me."

"You're bossy," she complains.

I arch a brow at her.

"Fine," she says, rolling her eyes at me. "He asked me out once right after I started working at the paper. I declined because he's kind of a dick. He acted like he was doing me a favor. Those were his actual words; he was just *trying to do me a favor*. I may not be a size three, but I'm not a pity date, which is precisely what I told him. He's been a jerk to me ever since. I think he wants me to fail so he can fire me."

"What the fuck?"

"He's a sexist jerk." She scowls at the television. "He tries to give all the women bullshit assignments and save the really meaty stuff for the male reporters. I think the only reason he agreed to let me interview you is because he expected me to fail." Her expression clears. "He was not happy when I told him you agreed to meet with me."

"Then he's going to be extra pissed when you hand over the story," I say, finding a certain savage satisfaction in that thought. Fuck Scarva for trying to touch what's mine and then for insulting her when she didn't go along with him. Men like him are precisely what is wrong with the world.

"About that..." Stella turns to face me, worrying her bottom lip between her teeth. "What if I didn't turn it in?"

"Why wouldn't you turn it in?"

She shrugs.

I see the little flash in her eyes, the split moment of unguarded, unflinching honesty. It rips through me like a bomb blast, setting off a landslide inside me. She would defy her boss, risk her job, and bury this story to protect the memory of a woman she didn't know. *For me.*

Does she know she's in love with me?

Cristo.

Is that what's happening between us? Is that why I can't keep my eyes off her?

Ever since she got here, I've been staring at her, unable to look away. I'm completely fucking gone over her. The thought of not having her here...stings. She's mine in a way that's permanent, unalterable. I would go to war for this girl, no questions asked.

"I didn't go into journalism to hurt anyone," she says, her voice soft. "I have enough to write a good profile on you without including Ana's story."

"Why?" I ask, hitting the power button on the remote to turn off the television.

She takes a breath. "Because this was never really about the story."

"Explain."

"You might not like it," she warns me.

"Stella, explain."

"Fine," she huffs and then mumbles something under her breath, which I assume is her calling me bossy again. As if she has any right to talk. She's a bossy little thing herself. Every time she gets fired up, I want to slide inside her and fuck her raw. "I've had a massive crush on you ever since that day in high school, and not knowing why you walked away from football was driving me crazy, so I pitched the story idea to Scarva because I'm nosy!"

I stare at her for a minute, take in her wide eyes and guilty expression. And then I chuckle. She really is curious about every-fucking-thing on the planet. "So you decided to interview me because you have a crush on me?"

"Who said I have a crush on you?"

"You did," I remind her, smiling.

"We're not talking about that!" she whisper-shouts.

I stare at her for a full five count, and then I laugh. This girl. *Cristo.* I can't deal with how fucking adorable she is.

She growls and launches herself at me. I catch her before she can smother me with a throw pillow and tumble her over backward, my hand behind her head to keep it from bouncing against the cushion. She stares up at me, her cheeks bright red and her hazel eyes wide. Even embarrassed, she's fucking beautiful.

"Promise me something," I murmur, brushing strands of her hair away from her face.

"What?"

"Never change."

"Clothes? Why? Can you see my nipples through my shirt?" She lifts her head slightly as if to check for herself.

"Fuck yeah, I can," I mutter, gently pushing her back down flat. "But I didn't mean the clothes, dimples. I meant you. Never change. You're perfect."

"Oh," she whispers, her body melting into the couch beneath me. Her expression softens, her eyes flitting across my face. I'm not sure what she sees there, but those bottomless eyes strip me bare, laying open all the parts of me that I've never shared with anyone, never wanted to share with anyone before now.

"What are you doing to me?" I ask her, aching for...something. Some reason or explanation as to why my world makes a hell of a lot more sense with her laid out beneath me than it did before she burst into my life like a comet. I barely know her, and yet...I think I know her better than anyone ever has. I think she knows *me*, sees me, more clearly than anyone ever has.

I've always believed in love. Of course I have. But this feels like something more. Fate or destiny or whatever it is that sweeps you along with it and takes no prisoners. It's fast and intense and addictive. I want this girl to love me. I want her to ache for me. I want her to see me every time she closes her eyes. I want to own her, possess her, make her as crazy as she makes me, so she never sees another man or thinks about one. Her world will begin and end with me.

I'm pretty fucking certain mine is already reordering itself to revolve around her. Every time she looks at me with those bottomless eyes, the spark between us blazes hotter and burns brighter. Every time she flashes those dimples, I fall a little harder. If I can't convince her to stay, she's going to rip my heart out of my chest when she goes.

"I don't know," she whispers back. "What are you doing to me?"

Do I tell her? Is it too soon? Fuck it.

"Making you fall in love with me," I mutter, dipping my head to touch my lips to hers. I kiss each corner and then flick my tongue against the seam, demanding she let me in.

She submits with a whimper I feel all the way into my soul. Her arms slide around my neck, her legs around my waist. I lose myself in her, running my hands all over her body. She's soft everywhere, her body pliant. It's been a decade since I touched a woman, but this doesn't feel anything like that.

For the first time in my life, it feels *right*. She's the one I've been waiting for, the reason I stopped dating. The reason I spend my days writing about something I've never had. She's a piece of me, some tangible, vital part I need. I think some part of me knew it that day at her school. I think I've been subconsciously waiting for her to grow up and come to me every day since. She wasn't ready for me then. I wasn't ready for her then. We both had to grow up and find ourselves. But I think some part of me recognized even then that she was going to change my life.

"Adrian," she whispers against my lips, her voice soft and sweet. "Make love to me."

I pull back slightly to look at her. Her lips are swollen from my kisses, her cheeks flushed. But those hazel eyes are full of certainty.

"I want you to be my first," she says, holding my gaze.

"If I get inside you, I'll be more than just your first, Stella," I growl, making sure that shit is clear here and now. "Once I'm in you, you're mine."

"Will you be mine?" she asks, a challenge in her expression.

"Already am," I mutter. "Once you're in my bed, there won't be anyone else for either of us."

She reaches up, tracing my lips with her fingertips. "I think it's too late for that already," she whispers, watching me carefully. "It feels like it's already been decided, doesn't it?" Her teeth sink into her plump bottom lip for a split second. "I think I've been yours since I was sixteen, Adrian."

"I think you might be right," I grunt, pressing a hard kiss to her mouth. "You kept me waiting long enough, *docinho*."

"Aww, poor football star. Did you get bored of your hand waiting for me?" she sasses, her lips curved into a smile.

"You're a savage little thing," I mutter, chuckling. I love how feisty she is. She doesn't give an inch without making me pay for it. That's all right, though. I'll gladly pay whatever price she demands so long as it means she's mine. And I fully intend to make her pay too. With sweat and cum and my handprints on her gorgeous ass.

I've never laughed as much with someone as I have with her. She has a response for everything and gives me shit when it suits her. I love how she goes from giving me hell to shy in the blink of an eye. All I have to do is look at her and she's trembling and blushing. Scarlet may be my new favorite color.

I lean down to kiss her again, deeper this time. She mewls into my mouth, wrapping herself around me like a blanket. I love the way she clings to me as if she's never letting me go. Her arms are locked tight around my neck, her legs around my waist. I can feel the heat coming off her pussy, smell her arousal.

"Up," I growl, lashing my arms around her to anchor her body to me while I climb to my feet. As soon as I'm steady, my mouth finds hers again. I nip her bottom lip before sucking it into my mouth to play with it.

She squirms in my arms, moaning.

Somehow, I manage to stop kissing her long enough to carry her to the bedroom. The hallway is almost pitch black. The storm still rages outside, lashing the coast with savage gusts of wind and torrential rain. We're in our own world out here, isolated and insulated from everyone else. It's just me and her.

I love everything about that.

I love *her*. It's fast, but it feels right, as if this was always supposed to happen. There is a reason I never forgot her, a reason I agreed to let her interview me. It was supposed to be her. I just didn't know it until today.

I know it now, with every fiber of my being. This feisty little goddess is mine, and I'm not ever letting her go.

CHAPTER SEVEN
STELLA

By the time Adrian carries me into his bedroom, I'm trembling. With excitement. With nerves. I hardly know which I feel more. All I know for sure is that I've never wanted anything more than I want this.

"You're shaking, *docinho*," he murmurs, laying me out in the center of his bed. One big hand slides down my body from shoulder to hip, leaving a trail of fire and gooseflesh in its wake. "Are you scared to be mine?"

"No." I've never been *less* afraid of something in my life.

"Good girl." He smiles at me before leaning back to strip his shirt off over his head. And holy crap. I thought I was prepared after this morning, but he's just as impressive the second time around. I've seen statues softer than him. Every ridge of his abdomen is clearly defined, so are his pecs. His arms are corded with muscle. He's so damn beautiful.

"How much time do you spend at the gym?" I ask.

"More questions?"

I swallow hard, nervous all over again. "Fair warning, but I do *not* look like that under these clothes."

"Thank God," he says, his expression soft. It sobers when I roll my eyes at him. "I'm not them, baby. I know men...*boys*...like you've dealt with haven't done right by you. They didn't treat you like the miracle you are, but I'm not them. Your body is a work of art, Stella. It's the reason for this." He grips his erection through his jeans, squeezing it.

I press my thighs together, the ache between them intensifying. "Adrian," I whisper...moan, really. My nerves settle. He wants me exactly the way I am. I'm not sure how this is my life, but I'm not questioning it anymore.

"I'm big and hard everywhere, dimples. And you were built to take me." He runs his gaze down my body, his eyes heating. "When I'm fucking the air out of your lungs, you'll know it too."

Oh, jeez.

I like his filthy mouth a lot.

"Show me."

"My dick? Plan on it, baby. Repeatedly."

"Not that." I pause. "Not *only* that," I correct, which makes him grin at me. "Show me what you said."

"Stand up."

"Bossy."

He quirks a brow, silently commanding me to obey him. Like usual, I do. I can't help it. When he looks at me like that, I *need* to obey him, for reasons I'm only just discovering. When he rewards me with that grin or calls me a good girl, I feel like I'm flying.

I've always been headstrong and easily excited. It wasn't just my weight people targeted. It was everything about me. I was loud and messy, too much of all those things women aren't supposed to be. I'm not too much for Adrian. Everything they hated about me, he seems to love.

I sit up, allowing him to pull me to my feet. He brushes his lips across my temple before turning me in his arms to face the giant doors.

We reflect back in the dark glass, him, standing like a warrior at my back. Me, trembling and wide-eyed in his arms. There's something captivating about the way we fit together, not as two individual pieces, but as one whole, as if we were made to fit exactly like this. We're not two disparate people, a gorgeous author, and a messy journalist. We're equals, perfectly crafted to fit together.

He slides his arms around my waist, kissing all over my neck as he lifts my shirt.

"Adrian," I whisper.

"Watch yourself, Stella," he murmurs. "See yourself like I do."

I'm not sure exactly what he wants me to see, but I bite back the automatic denial and nod. He rewards me with another kiss to my throat. Little by little, he lifts my shirt, exposing my body.

"You're so soft here," he murmurs, seaming his body to my back. His knuckles run over my belly, indicating what he means. "I love that softness, *docinho*. It's so fucking sexy to me." He fists my shirt in one hand, running the other across my wide hips. "These were made to cradle my body. To help you carry my kids."

"K-kids?" I stutter, my voice strangled.

"You think I'm putting a piece of latex between us when I get in you?" He cocks a brow, all bossy and authoritative again. "Told you already, dimples, once I'm in you, we're permanent."

He did tell me that. I guess I didn't think he meant *permanent* permanent though. But even in the dark glass,

I can tell he means exactly that. He wants a future with me, a family.

"I've always wanted babies," I whisper, my throat bone dry. My heart thumps an unsteady rhythm. I never had siblings growing up. I didn't have many friends, either. All my life, I've wanted a big family so my kids didn't grow up lonely like I did.

"Good," he mutters. "I'll give you as many babies as you want." He groans, pressing his face against the side of my throat. "I'll give you anything you want. Anything."

"I just want you, Adrian."

"You already have that," he says, all sweet and soft. And then he slips right back into bossy mode. "Eyes on the glass, *meu coração*. Watch what I do to you and how beautiful you look."

I tremble again, my eyes locked on the glass. He tugs my shirt the rest of the way up my body and then pulls it off over my head. I shiver when it lands on the floor at my feet. He growls at the same time, pressing more insistently into me from behind.

"So fucking sexy," he mutters, sliding his hands up my abdomen to cup my breasts. They overflow his big hands, the tops spilling out of the black lace demicups. I'm glad I put on a good bra this morning when I changed instead of a boring one like usual. He seems to appreciate the effort.

He kneads my flesh in his hands, soft at first and then rougher. His palms chafe my nipples, turning them into hard points that are visible even in the dark glass. I moan, melting into the hard wall of his chest as he plays with them.

"These tits drive me fucking crazy," he growls. "I can't wait to get my mouth all over them."

"What's stopping you?" I gasp.

He bites my neck and pinches my nipple at the same time, punishing me with pleasure. The way my clit pulses makes me want to keep being mouthy just so he keeps punishing me the same way. I'm like Milner's rats in the Skinner box, eager to push the button again and again to deliver that little jolt to my system.

"Lean forward," Adrian demands, gently nudging me until I do what he says. He makes quick work of the clasp on my bra, his deft fingers undoing it in one quick move-ment. His hands on my breasts are the only things keeping it in place. He slowly peels it away from my body, leaving me naked from the waist up.

I fight the instinctive urge to cover myself.

"There isn't a spot on you that doesn't make my dick throb, Stella," he growls, covering my bare breasts with his hands.

I cry out, surprised at how good it feels to have his skin against mine. And then I cry out again when he pinches both nipples. He leaves me gasping as he torments me, his eyes locked on me in the glass as if he can't look away. Nothing but pleasure reflects in his gaze. It makes me bolder, braver. I reach up, curving my arm around his neck to lock our bodies together.

His erection digs into my back. He's so hard. It has to be painful.

"I want to see the rest of you," he says, his hands questing down my abdomen again. One cups my center, his grip as possessive as the look in his eyes. "This is mine now, dimples. No one else sees it. No one else touches it."

"N-no one," I agree. Keeping that promise won't be a problem. No one has ever seen or touched me there, except my gyno. And he's seen enough vajayjay in his sixty-odd years that he probably doesn't think mine is all that memorable.

Adrian grinds his palm against me, making me cry out his name again.

"Fuck, I like it when you're all needy and begging, *docinho*. That little hitch in your voice drives me crazy." He makes quick work of the button on my slacks. The zipper isn't much of a barrier for him either. He shoves his hand in my pants, impatient and greedy to touch me.

"Adrian!" My legs turn to rubber. I latch onto his arms to keep myself upright as they threaten to tumble me to the floor.

"You're soaked," he growls, working his finger back and forth over the seam of my panties. And I know he's not kidding. I can practically hear how wet I am as he teases me. I feel how slick my folds are and the dampness on my thighs.

"It's your fault," I huff, not sure if I'm supposed to be this wet or not.

"Watch yourself, Stella," he says. "Look at how fucking beautiful you look." He presses his lips to my shoulder, his eyes meeting mine in the glass. "Your skin turns the prettiest pink when you need to come, dimples."

I can't see that in the mirror, but I see how wide my eyes are, and the way my lips are parted, waiting for me to moan again. I can't seem to stop the sound as he plays with me. The air has cooled since night fell. I feel it against my overheated skin, and it feels like heaven. He feels like heaven, too, wrapped around me like he never plans to move away.

He slides my panties to the side and touches my clit with his thumb.

My legs tremble again, threatening to give out. He lash-es his other arm around my waist, holding me upright.

I watch him in the mirror, see the way his hand moves, the way his expression grows darker and then darker still. Every time I moan, he growls, a triumphant sound I feel everywhere.

"I need to see all of you," he mutters in warning. Half a second later, my pants and panties are pooled at my feet. He doesn't even stop what he's doing to me either. He just yanks them down with his free hand in one quick tug.

"*Damn, amorzinho,*" he groans when I step out of them. "You really are beautiful everywhere. I've never seen anything as sweet as you."

"Adrian," I whisper, a lump in my throat. The way he talks to me, the awe in his voice...I can't help but believe him. Every dip and curve and roll of my body, every little imperfection or flaw, he finds worthy of admiration. This gorgeous, bossy man with his painful past and grumpy attitude, and perfect body finds me beautiful, inside and out. In the dark, with his eyes on me, for the first time in my life, I *feel* beautiful.

Is it too soon to love him this fiercely? If it is...too bad.

"Make love to me," I plead, needing him inside me before the way I feel manages to tear me apart. It's so strong, so powerful, like a riptide threatening to drag me under the waves. I've never felt anything like it before. It's beautiful and terrifying and somehow perfectly right all at once.

"Lean forward and put your hands on the glass," he says, walking me forward until I'm all but pressed up against it. If anyone is outside in the storm, they see all of me.

The glass is cool against my overheated skin. I shiver as my nipples come into contact with it. Before I can ask Adrian what he's doing, he drops to his knees behind me. I feel his breath on my bare ass, and the question dies in my throat.

I whimper, my hands turning to claws on the glass as he places both of his hands on my ass. He smacks my right cheek, groaning when I feel it bounce.

"Adrian!" I cry out, shocked when he sinks his teeth into the left one, biting me.

"I'm going to leave my marks all over this gorgeous ass," he growls and then smacks me again before he separates my cheeks and licks me.

My forehead thumps against the door, his name breaking from my lips in a loud cry as a sensation I've never felt rips through me.

"Oh my god," I moan, locking my legs to keep from falling over.

He buries his face in me from behind, a savage growl vibrating against my core. And my god, this is heaven. It has to be because there is no way pleasure like this exists on earth. It can't. We weren't made to withstand it.

"Adrian, Adrian," I gasp, trying to ask him what he's doing or what I'm doing or...something. I catch sight of myself in the glass and sob his name again. I look wrecked, my pupils so dilated they're all I can see. I watch myself as he eats me, using his lips and tongue to drive me wild.

His sounds and mine mix with the pattering of the rain and the way my hands slip and scrabble against the glass. With the sound of my heart trying to beat its way out of my chest. Everything seems brighter, bigger, and somehow less real at the same time, as if the only tangible things left in the world are the pleasure he's giving me and the way he holds me still as if he could eat me like this all night.

He definitely can't, though, because I'm not going to survive it. My body is already trembling as the first waves of an orgasm wash over me, unmaking me from the inside out. It's intense and powerful, roaring through me like a forest fire. It ignites every part of me, burns every little doubt, reservation, or fear out of existence in one fell swoop. All it leaves behind is need and *yes* and *please* and *more*.

And I know beyond a shadow of a doubt...he was right. There is no coming back from this. My body is his to command now, and only his. There won't ever be anyone else for me, or for him. For the rest of our lives, we're a unit, one soul, split between two bodies.

"There you are," he croons as I come back to myself. We're on the bed. Well, he's on the bed. I'm draped over him like a wanton sacrifice, every inch of my body damp with sweat and somehow still craving more. He's naked beneath me, his erection standing tall between us.

I knew he was big, but he's beautiful too. The head is red and engorged. Dark veins run down his shaft. The tip is slick with moisture. As soon as the desire to taste it on my tongue strikes, I reach out and swipe my finger across the tip, collecting a bead of it.

"Fuck," he growls, another bead welling from the slit when I touch my finger to my tongue. He's tangy, salty. It's an interesting combination, one I instantly love.

"Mm," I moan.

"You want me to fuck you raw?" he growls, narrowing his eyes on me. "Because you just squirted all over my face, and I'm hanging on by a thread here. You keep that up, you'll be on your back with my hand around your throat while you're screaming my name."

"Oh," I whisper, my core clenching hard.

"Fucking hell," he mutters, his eyes dark pools of fiery heat. "You're trying to kill me, aren't you?"

"No," I say, and then I giggle. "Maybe a little."

He growls wordlessly, and then his expression softens. "You came so hard, you damn near blacked out, dimples. You okay?"

"I'm...perfect." I smile. Yeah, that sounds right.

His smile matches my own. "Yeah, you are," he mutters, his voice gruff. He brushes my hair back from my face, running his hands up and down my back. "You're beautiful when you're coming, Stella."

"You make me beautiful."

"No, I make you happy. You've got the beauty part handled already."

"Adrian? Stop talking and make love to me now," I demand.

"Yes, ma'am," he says, chuckling. And then he sobers again, his eyes meeting mine. "I don't know how to make this easier for you, *docinho*. It's going to hurt like hell. I think you should be on top so you can control how fast we go, alright?"

"I..." I trail off and nod. "Help me. I don't know what to do." Admitting that to this gorgeous man makes me feel vulnerable in a way I never have before. He's so confident, so capable. I doubt there's anything he can't do.

"Me either," he says, shocking me. When I blink at him, he gives me a tender smile. "It's been a decade since I was last with anyone, Stella. And it wasn't like this. This is...us."

Satisfaction flares in his eyes when he says the word, as if he feels how right it is. "This is different."

"Adrian, I..."

"You love me," he says, stealing my thunder.

"I wanted to say it."

"Not until I do." He brushes my hair back from my face, smiles at me. "I love you, Stella Quinn. *Eu te amo*. I think I've been waiting for you my entire life."

"I love you too, Adrian," I whisper, moisture in my eyes. "I think I've loved you since I was sixteen."

His lips touch mine, soft and reverent. "Claim what's yours then, *meu coração*. Wrap that cunt around me and ride my cock."

How is it possible for him to be so sweet and filthy at the same exact time? For him to make me want to laugh and melt at once? I don't know, but it makes me love him even more. He's so many of the best things, all rolled into one. I love it so damn much.

If Scarva fires me, I think he'd be doing me a favor. I don't want to leave here. My life in Nashville is lonely and boring. I want to be here, making love to Adrian in his hideaway on the beach, laughing with him, loving him, *living* with him. I feel alive here, in ways I never even knew existed until today.

Maybe it's too soon or too fast, or we're completely crazy. That's okay. I'll be crazy for him. I'll be crazy with him. Because so long as he's by my side, I don't feel shame or as if we're moving too fast. I feel...free.

He shifts around until he's lounging against the headboard, all bossy and hot and naked. He helps lift me until I'm straddling his lap, his hands digging into my hips. My heart floats toward my throat, but I'm not nervous. I want to be his in every way.

"You're already killing me," he groans, rocking me back and forth. He's not the only one dying here. Every time his cock bumps my clit, I grow slicker, wetter, more turned on.

"God, Adrian," I moan, watching the way his abdomen clenches and his muscles ripple. If I could freeze time, it'd be right here and now, so I can look at him like this forever. His eyes are dilated, his cheeks flushed with desire. He looks like a warrior, so fierce and beautiful at the same time. He's sexy without even trying.

He notches his erection at my entrance, and I sink down on him slowly. My body resists him for a long moment. I want to sob in frustration. We're so damn close. I won't give up now. I can't. I need him in me. I think having him there is the only thing that's going to keep me from bursting apart at the seams.

"Fuck." His eyes roll back in his head when the head of his cock finally slips inside me.

Even that little bit leaves me breathless. He's so damn big, so hard. The way he stretches me burns. I already feel full of him. I sink down further, gasping as the burn intensifies.

"You're so fucking tight, dimples. Jesus. You're strangling my cock."

I grit my teeth, refusing to stop now. I take a deep breath, dig my nails into his muscular thighs, and slam myself down on him, ready to get the hard part over with. My hymen pops on the head of his cock, shearing in two. And holy crap. It hurts!

Adrian growls a curse, his hands turning into vises on my hips. His eyes fly open, landing on mine. I see every flicker of emotion that passes through them. Shock. Bliss. Anger.

"Adrian," I sob, writhing as the pain scorches its way through me. Tears pool in my eyes. It hurts like hell, but underneath the pain, there's something else. Joy. Awe. A sense of completeness I've never felt before. Even my dirtiest of dreams were a mere echo of the sense of rightness I feel knowing this part of me will always belong only to him. It's all-encompassing.

"Dimples," he breathes, leaning forward to wrap his arms around me. He holds me close, kissing away my tears.

His body trembles against mine, and I know how hard he's fighting to stay still and take care of me. He makes it seem easy as he runs his hands all over me, whispering to me and kissing all over my face. "Shh, *meu coração*. The hard part is over now."

"T-t-thank God," I sob, which makes him chuckle and then groan.

"I'd take the pain for you if I could," he murmurs, still kissing all over my face and touching me everywhere he can reach. "Are you okay, *docinho*?"

"No." I sniffle. "Yes. Jesus, Adrian. W-why are you so *big*?"

"You'll like me that way soon enough, Stella," he growls.

I take his word for it, figuring he's probably right. The pain is already flowing out, allowing pleasure to flow in. He feels good inside me. I'm stretched and full of him. I don't know how he fit inside me, but I'm pretty sure he was made to be there. Or I was made to fit him. Either way, I think I love the way he feels inside me.

"I need to move," I whisper.

"Then move, *docinho*. Ride me," he says, taking my lips in a deep kiss. His hands find my hips, fitting there as if they belong. He rocks me against him, making me moan. The same sound leaves his lips, breathed into my mouth.

We kiss and rock, moving together as he teaches me what to do. It doesn't take me long to catch on.

I use his thighs for leverage, lifting myself off him and then sinking back down. My hips roll, the movement instinctive. He seems to like it. His hands tighten on me, his breathing growing choppy, uneven. He breaks our kiss with a curse, leaning back against the headboard again.

"Work those hips and ride my cock, Stella," he says, his eyes at half-mast.

I give him what he wants, helpless to do anything but obey him. I lift off and drop down, taking him deep over and over again. My breasts bounce each time I impale myself on him. He watches them before his gaze drops lower, fixated on the sight of him disappearing inside me again and again.

"That's it," he growls. "Keep taking my dick like you need it to survive."

I do, bouncing on his lap harder, faster, taking him deeper. His cock hits a spot inside that has my head lolling on my shoulders and my entire body clenching. I sob his name. I didn't know it would be like this. All my dreams, all my fantasies, all the books I read...they never got this part quite right. Or maybe they did, and I just didn't have a standard of measure.

"Adrian," I whimper when he hits that spot again. I lose my rhythm. Lose everything. My core clenches, my inner muscles clamping down around him. I come in a heated rush of pleasure, gasping at how sudden and consuming it is. My body liquifies, turns to smoke.

As soon as he feels it, he growls and tumbles me backward off his lap, coming down over me. My head is at the foot of the bed, but he doesn't seem to mind. He yanks my leg up over his hip, opening me up to him. And then he takes charge, fucking me hard and deep. He told me this morning that he was going to wreck me. He wasn't lying.

He fucks me like he can't stop himself. He's a machine, relentless as he fucks me higher and higher, leaving me floating in some level of nirvana that rivals heaven. His teeth close over my nipple. He bites and licks and sucks, growling as he puts his mouth all over both of them just like he said he would.

"You aren't going to be able to walk tomorrow, Stella," he growls, almost as if he's mad about it. "*Cristo*. I'm going to fuck you through the floor if you don't stop me."

"Don't," I gasp. "Don't stop. Never stop."

"Stella."

"Please, please don't stop," I beg, shameless as another orgasm ignites deep in my belly.

He roars my name, flipping me over onto my stomach.

I cry out, but before I can even miss him, he yanks my hips up high and slams back inside me. I sob his name, stunned at how much deeper he is this way. He pounds into me, his balls slapping against my ass hard enough to sting. His hips crash into mine again and again.

"So fucking sexy," he growls, smacking my ass again.

Even that feels good. Too good, maybe.

"Look at the way this ass bounces," he says and then smacks it again. "I'll be fucking it soon too, Stella. That mouth and those tits too. I'm going to cover you in cum, make you wear it so everyone knows you belong to me."

"Yes," I sob, more than willing to wear him all over me.

He smacks my ass again and then wraps one arm around my waist, pulling me up to my knees. His lips land against my throat, his kiss sweet. His hand inches down my belly, sliding between my thighs. He touches my clit, making me sob and writhe. The only thing keeping me upright is the way he's holding onto me.

"Come for me again, *docinho*," he croons, pulling my lobe into his mouth. "Let me feel you soaking me while I'm claiming that womb."

I want to deny him because I know if I come again, it's going to wreck me. But I can't. Whatever he wants, I'll give him. I can't help myself. He's part of me, the piece that's been missing for my entire life. I can't deny him.

"Adrian," I sob, overwhelmed with pleasure and love. God, I feel like I'm drowning in it. And I still want more. No, not more. I want everything he has. Until he's wrecked like I am, ruined for anyone but me. I've never been greedy or selfish before. I've never wanted anything badly enough to covet it. But I want him that way. I need him that way.

"Come, Stella," he growls. "Give it to me, *meu coração*."

I wail his name into the room, screaming it in defiance, in surrender. My body locks down on his. I think my heart stops beating. Everything goes black for a split second, and then the entire world lights up. I come hard, screaming, clawing, begging.

"Stella! God, *amorzinho*," he growls, his voice a dark rasp. His body goes rigid behind me, a guttural cry escaping in a burst of sound that's almost painful to hear. He comes in a flood of heat and broken groans. I feel each one like a kiss, branding me with his name, with his seed.

We writhe together, a tangle of limbs and bliss and sweat and cum, clinging to one another as it unmakes both of us, puts us back together in some incredible new order. *Us,* just like he said. Somehow, it's better than perfect.

We collapse in a heap, gasping for breath, trembling. He pulls me into his arms, holding me tight as we try to come down. He kisses me between panted breaths, worshipping me with his lips and hands. He whispers my name like a prayer.

"*Eu te amo, docinho. Eu te amo.* You did so good. God, I'm still shaking."

"Me too," I whisper.

And then I sleep, safe and sheltered in his arms.

CHAPTER EIGHT
STELLA

I wake up close to midnight, but Adrian isn't in the bed with me. I sit up, slightly worried that maybe I read more into what happened between us than I should have. He said all the right things, or maybe I just thought they were the right things?

What am I thinking? He loves me. I know he loves me.

I'm just being crazy.

I hop up, stealing his t-shirt off of the floor to cover myself. I wince as soon as I take a step, sore in places I didn't know I could be sore. It's a delicious reminder of what he did to me, of the way he made me feel. Lord, I knew he was hot, but I did not know he was unrepentantly wicked.

Just thinking about the way he felt inside me makes my stomach flutter and heat flow through me. I want to do it again and again.

Rain still patters against the skylight and the roof, though it's far less savage now. I think the storm is finally moving on. I don't particularly relish the thought of being able to leave here. I'm not due back in Nashville until Monday, but I like being here with Adrian. I feel different with him...like a woman instead of a hot mess. He makes me feel sexy and desired, two things I've never felt in my life.

He also makes me so freaking happy I could float away.

"Adrian?" I call softly, stepping out into the hall.

He doesn't answer, but I hear a familiar tapping sound and smile. He's writing.

I follow the sound down the hall, peeking my head in his office to find him at the desk, his dark head bent over his laptop. He's shirtless, all that golden-brown skin on display.

The claw marks down his arms have my cheeks heating. Maybe I'm a little wicked too.

His office is interesting. One entire wall is full of book-shelves. There are trophies and awards scattered around the shelves alongside more pictures of him and his mom, and him with his foster sisters. I think Ana is the older of the two girls. She's thin and willowy, with a shy smile and pretty eyes. Her little sister is equally as beautiful, though there's a hint of mischief in her smile.

The French doors that open onto the deck are closed tight.

I watch him for a long moment, smiling. He's in his own world, completely focused on whatever story is playing out in his mind. His mouth moves every once in a while, as if he's murmuring the words out loud. He types fast. His hands practically fly across the keys. Watching him work is a sort of intimacy I didn't expect. I instantly fall in love with it.

He stops typing suddenly and glances up, his eyes locking on me.

I fight the urge to fidget as he looks me over, his obsidian eyes growing darker.

"Hi," I whisper.

"You look good in my shirt, dimples," he murmurs, holding out a hand toward me. There's so much command in the move, as if he expects me to obey. It's autocratic, hot.

I cross toward him, allowing him to pull me down onto his lap.

"You weren't in bed."

"That's because you were trying to kick me out of it," he says with a chuckle. "You're wild in your sleep."

"I wake up every morning tangled up in my blankets," I admit. "My cat won't even sleep with me anymore."

"You have a cat?"

"Gollum." I smile. "He hates everyone and everything except the broom. Whenever he sees it, he loses his little mind, wanting me to sweep him. I think he's obsessed with it."

Adrian chuckles.

"What are you working on?" I ask, glancing at his laptop screen. The page he has open is mostly blank, making it impossible for me to be nosy and read whatever he's writing.

His lips touch my shoulder. "I woke up inspired," he murmurs. One hand slides down my stomach, inching my shirt up.

"Yeah?" I whisper, my whole body clenching in anticipation as his hand creeps lower.

"Are you sore, *docinho*?" He cups my pussy in his palm and then runs his thumb across my slit before pressing it to my clit.

"N-no," I lie, arching my hips to get closer to his hand.

"You are." His brows furrow. "I should let you rest."

"No," I whisper. "Tell me what you're working on."

"You want to read it?"

I shake my head, my cheeks heating. He notices.

"You want me to read it to you." He smiles, a wolfish, wicked smile. His thumb jiggles my clit, making me whimper. He releases his grip on me with the other, reaching out to scroll back to what he was writing.

"*My hands slide down his abs like water falling, my eyes locked on his in a connection so deep, I can't breathe,*" he reads, draping my legs over the arms of his chair to open me up to him.

I shiver, my blood rapidly heating.

He touches me again, sliding his fingers through my folds as if he knows exactly what I need.

"*'Take it,' he groans, wrapping his hands in my hair. His hips thrust forward, the head of his cock slipping past my lips and into my eager mouth.*"

Oh my god.

"*I moan at the sensation,*" he murmurs, sliding one finger inside me. He curls it up, touching my g-spot. "*It's all smooth, hard heat, and I want it. Every inch, until my eyes water. Until I can't breathe. I don't want it slow. I don't want to be in control. I want him like only I know he can be: forceful, demanding… fucking my mouth until I can't take any more.*"

"Adrian," I whimper, riding his hand as his voice and what he's doing to me send me reeling out of this dimension.

"'Yes,' he grunts, reading the plea in my eyes," he says in that wicked voice. His thumb presses against my clit again. *"His fist tightens in my hair. He thrusts forward faster. Harder. Deeper."*

I tremble in his arms, drenching his hand.

"I'm dripping wet, moaning around the length of his cock as his eyes fall closed and his head kicks back. Little grunts fall from his lips," he reads, flicking my clit and stroking my g-spot at the same time.

I cry out his name into the dark, coming hard.

"Mine are stretched wide in silent bliss," he whispers, pressing his mouth to mine to swallow my cries. He works me through it, not letting up even when I gasp and whimper. *"That's just fine with me, though...we both know I'll have plenty of reason to scream later."*

"Adrian," I whimper.

He chuckles and then kisses me long and deep, bringing me slowly back down to earth. I land in his arms, blissed out and smiling.

"You should narrate your books," I mumble, cuddling up in his arms.

"Yeah?" He chuckles again, sliding his hand from between my legs. He pops his fingers into his mouth, cleaning my juices from them. And lord, that's hot.

"Settle down," he murmurs, swatting me gently on the thigh when I squirm. "You'll make me forget you're sore, *docinho.*"

"I'm not very sore."

"Liar." He kisses me again, soft and sweet.

We cuddle for long moments, both content just to be together.

"The storm is over," he says a few minutes later. "The road should be passable by late afternoon."

"Oh," I whisper, disappointment filling me. Nervous energy does too, snapping me wide awake. I'm not ready to leave.

"When are you supposed to fly back to Nashville?"

"The day after tomorrow. Um, Saturday." It's not enough time.

"It's not enough time," he mutters, echoing my thoughts.

"I know." My heart twists in my chest, tears pooling in my eyes. "What are we going to do, Adrian? Your life is here, and mine is there. I don't know what to do."

"Do you...want to leave?"

"I have a job. And a cat." I've never hated working for Scarva as much as I do right now. It would be so easy to make the decision to stay if I didn't have a job and actual adult responsibilities waiting for me. But I can't afford not to work.

"Come on," Adrian says, securing his arms around me before he rises to his feet.

He holds me close to his chest, carrying me through his office. He hits the light on the way out before turning down the dark hall toward his bedroom. Once we're in the bed again, he strips his shirt off over my head, throwing it over the side. The sweats he donned after climbing from the bed follow it. And then I'm back in his arms, my head against his chest.

"What if you had a job here?" he asks.

"I don't."

"You could," he says. "I own a newspaper, dimples."

"Adrian, I..."

"Think about it," he whispers, urgency in his voice. "You wouldn't have to deal with that Scarva fucker. You could pick your own stories, decide what you write and when."

I hesitate for a long moment, dying to say yes, but also slightly terrified to take that step. What if I do and he gets tired of me? What if he regrets it later? I already love him so damn much. But we're moving at the speed of light. The thought of him changing his mind is unbearable.

"You hate the idea."

"I don't hate the idea," I disagree, my voice soft. "I'm just...scared."

"Of what?" He rolls until I'm on my back with him hovering over me. Even in the silvery light filtering in through the skylight and windows, he's gorgeous. "Talk to me, *docinho*."

"We're already moving so fast. What if you change your mind about me?"

"Ah, *amorzinho*," he croons. "You think I could learn to unlove you? To not want to spend every waking moment with you?" He dips his head to rest his forehead against mine. "I've never been more certain of anything than I am of this, Stella. Of you. I know it's frightening. You've been neglected your entire life by people who weren't worthy of you. But I'm not them, *docinho*. There isn't a single thing about you that I don't love. I'm not going anywhere."

"Adrian," I whisper around the lump in my throat.

"You belong with me, Stella," he whispers, brushing his nose across the side of mine. His lips seek mine in the quasi-darkness, his kiss as sweet as his words. "The only way I can prove that to you is if you take a leap of faith with me, dimples. But I won't push you. If you don't want to stay, I won't ask you to give up your entire life for me."

"W-what are you saying?" I ask.

"I'm saying...Nashville is nice this time of year. It's been a long time since I had a reason to leave Spring."

"You'd come to Nashville with me?"

"I'd pitch a tent in hell if that's what you wanted, dimples," he says, bumping his nose against mine again. "This may be fast and crazy, but I don't give a fuck. You're mine. I told you before you let me in that hot little cunt that we're permanent. That hasn't changed. I'm going wherever you go."

"I love it here," I whisper. Only Adrian could surround something so filthy with words sweet enough to make me cry. He holds nothing back, reserves no part of himself. From the minute I arrived, he's given me his truth, his pain, his heart, everything. It's my turn to give a little. "I have to go back to Nashville."

"Then I'll go with you," he says simply, as if it doesn't matter to him in the least if we go or stay so long as we're together.

"I mean, I have to go back to Nashville to pack."

He freezes, barely even breathing.

"I hope you're not allergic to cats," I whisper, smiling so big it hurts my cheeks.

"You're moving in with me."

"Well, I...I guess I didn't think about where I would stay," I say, feeling a little sheepish. "But yes. If you'll have me, this is where I want to be. Right here with you."

"That wasn't a question, *docinho*. You're moving in with me. There are too damn many single men in this town," he mutters. "I'm going to keep you tied to this bed until you're pregnant, just so they all know you're off limits."

"Adrian," I say, laughing. He's completely crazy and completely serious. And I love him so damn much for being both.

He shifts, causing his cock to nudge my belly.

I moan when I feel it, and then push on his shoulders. "Roll over," I demand.

"Bossy," he teases. He also gives me what I want, flopping over onto his back.

I crawl over him, kissing my way down his chest and abdomen. I wrap my hand around his erection, marveling at how hard he is and how big. I can barely fit my fingers around him. I have no idea how I'm going to fit him in my mouth, but I'm going to make it work one way or another.

"What are you doing, dimples?" he asks, his voice gritty, his lips lifting from the bed.

"Inspiring you again."

"Fuck yeah," he whispers.

CHAPTER NINE
ADRIAN

"I'm proud of you, *irmão*," Camila says, a smile in her voice.

"Yeah?" I pace in the lobby of Stella's work building, impatient to see her again. Worried about her facing Don Scarva without me. She insisted on doing it alone, though. And as much as I want to break his face with my fist, I wouldn't dream of stealing her thunder today. She's been looking forward to this meeting since she finished writing her article on Friday. Hell, I think she's been looking forward to it since he asked her out when she first started.

She's turning in her profile on me and her resignation.

I'm not sure how I feel about the world knowing Ana's name, but Camila was right. It's time for the world to hear her story. Stella wanted to leave her out of the profile. She said some secrets are worth keeping, but I told her to include it. It's beyond time. I'm not naïve enough to believe it will change anything in the world of professional sports. They'll close ranks and protect their own like always. But others will hear it. Others will change because of it.

I did. In ways I never expected. Losing my foster sister taught me who I wanted to be, and who I would never be. Throwing a football down a field...there's glory there for a lot of men. But there is no heart. At least, not for me. Who I am now, what I do now...I'm proud of that man. I don't know if I could have changed what happened to Ana, but I've made a difference for others. That's worth more than any contract or endorsement deal. To me, that's enough.

If Ana's story inspires change for anyone else, the world will be better off for it. And if that doesn't happen...at least the world will know her name. They'll know that Derrick Lovelace wasn't a hero. They'll know the bright girl with the shy smile who had big dreams and a bigger heart.

Stella didn't know the story waiting for her when she came to me, but I can think of no one I'd rather have tell Ana's story than her. There is no one I trust with her memory more than my little water Nymph.

"Adrian!" Camila shouts into the phone. "Are you listening to me?"

"Sorry, no."

"Are you regretting your decision?" she asks, instantly solicitous.

"No. I was just thinking," I murmur.

"About Ana?"

"And about Stella."

"I can't wait to meet her."

"You'll love her," I say, smiling. They're a lot alike. Camila is hell on wheels like Stella. And equally as stubborn and bossy when she wants to be.

"I already love her. Are you kidding me? She got your crabby ass out of Spring. She's a goddess as far as I'm concerned. *Mamãe* agrees with me."

"We're going back to Spring," I remind her, stopping to glance out the window. We're on the bottom floor of one of the high-rises downtown. The wind is fierce. It rips a newspaper out of an elderly man's hand and sends it flying down the street. He stops walking and shakes a fist at it as if cursing heaven. Two young girls chase after it, trying to catch it for him. I think that ship has sailed, though. Pages are scattering every which way, some lifted high as they blow away.

"Maybe, but you actually left for once," Camila says. "You must really like her."

"She's my one."

"I love you, and I'm so happy for you, but if anything the two of you do together inspires your books, I swear to God, we're never speaking again, Adrian," she says. "I do not need to know some things."

"You aren't allowed to read my books anyway," I mutter. "You aren't old enough."

"I'm twenty-four."

"Still not old enough."

Camila laughs at me. "You're such a prude."

"Tell that to Stella," I say, smirking.

"I'm hanging up on you now," Camila singsongs. "Call me later. Love you. Bye."

I chuckle when she disconnects before I can say anything else. I stare out the window for a minute before turning to glance at the doors to the elevator. It's only been half an hour since they carried Stella upstairs, but it feels like a lifetime.

This is the longest we've been apart since she fell into my arms last week. I can't wait to get her back to her place and get her naked again. She belongs on my cock, at least for the next seventy years. The way she takes me...my god, she's a greedy little thing. When she starts begging, I lose it. Every damn time.

I never knew sex could be this incredible, or that simply holding someone would feel so good. My life is so much brighter because Stella is in it. Those sexy dimples, her wide eyes, the wild shit she says...every minute with her is an adventure. I'm dying to get my ring on her finger.

I know she wants a traditional wedding. I'm more than happy to give her that. Whatever she wants. But when we get back to her place, I'm putting a ring on her finger. Maybe then the thought of her being around so many fucking men when we get back to Spring won't piss me off so much. Though at the rate residents have been falling in love, maybe it won't be an issue much longer. We had two more engagement announcements come in at the paper today. They landed in my inbox damn near simultaneous-ly.

Stella is dying to get back to Spring and sort out the mystery. She insists it's simply not normal to have so many hot men—her words, not mine—all in one place. She's going to be pissed when I tie her to my bed to keep her away from them. It's the twenty-first century. They can answer her questions on the phone or over text. At least until she's pregnant with my kid. Which shouldn't be long if I keep getting in her like I have been.

Though, I'm not going to lie. As much as I love when she's wrapped around me, milking my cock...my favorite moment is right afterward. When she's cuddled up in my arms, purring like a little kitten. That sound lets me know she's happy, that I pleased her. It's replaced the ocean as my favorite sound. I feel like a God when she makes that sound.

The elevator dings. I pause in mid-pace.

"I did it!" Stella yells as soon as the doors slide open. She flings her hands up in the air and then realizes we aren't entirely alone in the lobby. She drops her arms back to her side, grimacing at the receptionist. "Sorry, Lorna."

The elderly receptionist shakes her head, smiling.

The doors to the elevator start sliding closed. Stella squeaks and rushes forward, squeezing her hand in between them. The doors open again. Stella hurries out of the elevator, her tits bouncing in her pretty dress. She always looks beautiful, but there's a lightness to her step and a satisfaction in her eyes that's new.

I pull her into my arms as soon as she's close enough for me to get my arms around her. She tips her head back, her lips parted as if to say something. I take them in a deep kiss. She kisses me back for a minute before making a squeaking sound and practically catapulting out of my arms.

"We're in public," she hisses.

"So?"

"You can't kiss me in public."

"Yeah, that's not going to work for me, dimples," I growl, reaching out to grab her.

She takes a quick step back. "No more kissing me," she says, slapping her hand over her lips to hide them from me. As if that'll stop me.

"I don't like this rule," I mutter, glaring at her.

Lorna hears me and chuckles.

"What did Scarva say?" I ask Stella, tugging her close to me again. There's something addictive about feeling her softness pressed up against me. It instantly soothes me.

"Surprisingly, not much," she says, pulling her hand away from her mouth. "But the look on his face was totally worth it. He looked like he stepped in poo and then walked across his carpet." She exhales a gusty breath. "I should have let Jenna record it."

"I like Jenna."

"Do you know Ian Sterling?" she asks me.

"We played together for a year. Why?"

"Do you know his brother?"

"Mac? We met a few times."

"I think Jenna is in love with Mac," she says, her eyes wide. "She's been all weird and secretive since she interviewed Ian. I finally got her to fess up. They've been seeing each other. Like s-l-e-e-p-i-n-g together seeing each other."

"Stella," I say, fighting laughter. "Lorna's in her sixties. She can spell."

"You're ruining my moment here, Adrian," she says.

Fuck, I love her.

"By all means, continue."

"I'm finished now." She stops pouting to smile at me. "We should go before Scarva sends security to escort me out."

"Don't you need to clean out your desk?"

"There's nothing in it." She shrugs almost sheepishly. "I took it all home once he threatened to fire me the first time. I figured it was only a matter of time."

I turn to glare at the elevators, weighing whether or not I want to go punch her former boss in the face or not. Doing it would almost be worth whatever shitstorm comes my way because of it. The fact that Stella has been living in fear of him pisses me off to no end.

"I'm ready to go home to Spring," she says, snuggling up against me. "I miss the beach. Let's go pack and get Gollum."

As soon as she calls my place home, the desire to punch Don Scarva in the face drains out of me. I make a mental note to have a buddy check into him and see what he can shake loose. He's not a threat to Stella anymore. My girl is free, and we're going home. But someone needs to deal with him before he tries the same shit on another woman.

"Yeah, *docinho*," I murmur, pressing my lips to her temple. "Let's get the fuck out of here."

Her answering smile is the best sort of closure. It's pure light.

"We're getting married!" Stella shouts a week later, leaning over the deck to shout her announcement to the ocean. The wind grabs her hair, flinging it all around. She laughs and bats it out of her face, trying to hold Gollum with the other hand.

He's less thrilled about the beach than she is. He hisses and takes a swipe at her.

"Here," I murmur, taking him from her arms before he claws her. As soon as he's in mine, he hisses again. I'm convinced the cat doesn't like anyone but Stella.

I set him inside the house and then pull the doors closed so he doesn't dart out. Call me crazy, but I'm guessing he's not going to be a big fan of sand, the ocean, or outside either. He's a grumpy little fucker. He wants to sleep, eat, and be left alone.

Once he's safely inside, I step up behind Stella, wrapping my arms around her. She melts against my chest, letting me hold her. I breathe her in, peaceful in ways I didn't know was possible.

Her profile on me published early this week. I thought it would be difficult to see it laid out in the paper but seeing Stella's byline and the care she took with it felt like a weight off my chest. It's a good feeling. For so long, I've lived with guilt and regret. It's...strange to finally feel peace. I never knew what that felt like before Stella. I never believed I deserved that before her.

People will say what they want to say about Ana's relationship with Lovelace. But the people who matter—the ones who knew and loved her—know the truth. What anyone else decides to believe is up to them. The narrative isn't mine to control, nor should it be. Stella's profile gave me an opportunity to share my truth. I hope like hell it gives others courage to do the same.

But if not...simply being able to honor Ana the way she deserves is enough.

"I have my first story for your paper," Stella murmurs, laying her head against my chest.

"Yeah?" I nuzzle her neck, placing kisses to the sensitive strip of skin behind her ear. "What's your story, dimples?"

"This town. You. Love." She peeks up at me, smiling. "There's magic here, Adrian."

"Magic?" I chuckle at her.

"Love is magic," she says with a shrug, undeterred. "At least it feels that way to me. I want to write about all the men here who have discovered that magic for themselves. Maybe it'll bring more women here to find their happily-ever-afters too. We can do profiles on everyone who is still single and searching."

I smile, not surprised this is what she wants to do. She's a journalist, full of curiosity. But she also wants everyone to be happy. I think she runs on love. If there's magic in this town, it's because she's here, shining like the sun.

The paper is hers. She can do what she wants with it. I always thought I only bought it to keep reporters from bothering me. But maybe there was a little bit of that magic of hers at work, preparing me for her when she finally found her way to me. Coincidences happen, but this seems a little like divine providence to me.

I scoop her up into my arms to carry her back inside.

"I wasn't finished staring at the ocean," she says, throwing her arms around me.

"Too bad," I mutter. "If you're writing about single men, we have shit to do."

"We do? Like what?"

"Getting you pregnant for starters, dimples."

"Oh," she whispers, her eyes lighting up. "I like this plan, Adrian."

"Yeah?" I grin, not telling her that part of said plan involves tying her to my bed. She'll find that out soon enough. Instead, I capture her lips with mine, pouring my complete fucking adoration into our kiss, until we're both gasping for breath. "I love you, Stella Quinn."

"That's because I'm awesome," she whispers, her expression soft.

I throw my head back and laugh.

"I love you too, Adrian," she says, sobering. She lifts a hand, cupping my cheek. "I love you so damn much."

"Smart girl," I murmur, kissing her again.

It's a long time before we come up for air this time.

It's even longer before I untie her from the bed.

Epilogue
STELLA

<u>Five Years Later</u>

"This is harder than it looks," I whisper to myself, trying to hold Adrian's arm up and fasten the tie around his wrist to the bedpost at the same time. Preferably without waking him up. I like spankings as much as the next girl, don't get me wrong. But I also like being able to walk, and with a four-year-old, a two-year-old, and a nine-month-old underfoot most days, being mobile is kind of necessary.

Granted, they're spending the weekend with Camila and her husband, Gray, but I still like being able to walk. And it never looks this complicated when Adrian ties me to the bed. Or maybe it only looks easy because I'm an active participant. He's sleeping.

In my defense, catching him asleep was the only way to get the ties on him. Every time I bring it up, he distracts me until I forget. I've come to the inevitable conclusion that all the distractions are intentional. He likes being the one in charge. *I* like him being in charge. But today, it's my turn.

Since I'm pregnant, he can't be mad at me. Well, he can be mad at me. But once I drive him crazy and tell him the news, he'll be fine.

It's been five years and he's as bossy as ever. But he's also the sweetest man I've ever met. When I'm pregnant, he's completely over-the-top. I've never met a man so excited to see his wife get bigger. He loves it, though. I know this because he can't keep his hands off me.

Even if he has to pull me into the pantry while the boys are watching cartoons or eat me on the washer while they're coloring, he finds a way to get me off every day. I'm not complaining. Sex with Adrian is incredible. He does the filthiest things to me.

At this point, I don't know how we've never been caught in the act. He's made love to me in the ocean, on the sand, on the deck, in his truck on the side of the road every time Billy, who lives in Spring, smiles at me. Billy is harmless, but Adrian swears he has a thing for me. He thinks the same thing about every man who smiles at me. He's completely crazy.

"Dimples?" he mumbles in his sleep.

I bite my lip and quickly tighten the tie around his wrist.

And not a second too soon. I barely have it cinched when he tries to move his arm. His dark brows crinkle, his eyes shifting behind his closed eyelids.

I sit back on my heels, waiting patiently for him to wake up and figure out what I did. My heart thumps unevenly. I'm not afraid of his reaction, though. He likes to punish me with pleasure because he's a wicked, wicked man.

I love every second of it. Our life together is magical. Every day, he finds a way to make me love him a little more. He's the best husband, friend, and father. Sure, he drives me crazy sometimes. He's bossy and grumpy and possessive. But I think he's perfect. He's mine, and I'm his and so long as we're together, it doesn't matter what we're doing or what's happening around us. I'm in heaven.

I know he is too. There's a light in his eyes that never goes out. He says that's because I make him so happy. I'll gladly take credit. Making my man happy makes me happy. He deserves it. He struggled for so long after losing his foster sister. I know he still misses her every day. It breaks my heart for him, for her, and for Camila and Áurea.

Adrian does so much for so many people and never shares a word of it. Not even his closest friends know that he funds women's shelters all over the state. He says he doesn't do it for credit but because it's the right thing to do. He's taught me so much about the kind of person I want to be in life. Our sons hero worship him...and they aren't the only ones. He is still my hero. Every single day.

He's more gorgeous than ever. At thirty-eight, he's still sexy as sin and built like a linebacker. I dread the day our boys grow up because I know they're going to look just like him. They're already mini replicas of him. We'll be beating girls off with a stick. I'm not worried about our boys breaking hearts, though.

Even though they're young, Adrian makes sure they know that women are meant to be cherished and treated with respect. He leads by example and treats me like a queen. Our boys imitate him. Lucas and André love to help him spoil me. Diego, the baby, isn't much help in that regard since he's only nine months old, but he spoils me with cuddles. He's the sweetest little baby, with big dimples and the curliest hair.

I really hope the new baby is a girl. I need another female in this house. Even Gollum is male. Surprisingly, he actual-ly likes the kids. I think old age is mellowing him. He even hangs out with Adrian in his office sometimes. I'm pretty sure Adrian bribes him with kitty weed, though. He denies this, but I'm suspicious.

Adrian tries to move his arm again only for the ties to stop him. His obsidian eyes spring open. "What the fuck?" he mumbles.

"Good morning, bossy," I say, fighting laughter as he tries to figure out why he can't move.

It doesn't take him long. He narrows his eyes on me and then cranes he head to examine my handiwork.

"Did you tie me to the bed, *docinho*?"

"Yes."

His long lashes flutter. He slowly turns to face me again. "Why?"

"You always tie me to the bed. It's my turn."

He regards me for a moment, looking all rumpled and sleepy and sexy. I swear, when he first wakes up, he's the sexiest thing I've ever seen. I fall a little harder for him every time he reaches for me without even opening his eyes in the morning. It lets me know I'm his very first thought.

"You want to have your way with me, dimples?" he rumbles. His cock stirs, hardening.

"Yes."

For a long moment, he just stares at me with those sleepy obsidian eyes. And then he grins, the most wicked, feral grin I've ever seen. If I were wearing panties, they'd be dust. "Then do what you will, *meu coração*. But when you untie me, *I* get to play," he murmurs, his voice still rough from sleep. "You're lucky the boys are with Camila for the weekend. Because you're going to scream the fucking roof down before I'm done with you."

"Happy anniversary to me," I say with a soft laugh. It doesn't feel like it's been five years since the day I invaded his beach to pepper him with questions. Sometimes, it feels like we've been together forever. Other times, it feels like no time at all has passed.

His expression softens. "*Eu te amo.*"

"I love you too." I run my hand down the side of his scruffy cheek and then grin. "Now behave. I have work to do."

"Start by sitting on my face," he demands, being all bossy even though he's tied up and at my mercy. Let's be honest, though, I could wrap him in chains, and he'd still be in charge. That's just who he is, and I love him for it. "I haven't had breakfast yet."

"Maybe I'll let you have it. Later." I scoot down the bed until I'm kneeling at his side. His cock is standing straight up now, impatiently waiting for me to give him attention. I slide my hands down his abs, lightly scraping him with my nails.

He growls my name, his hips arching up from the bed.

I stop inches from his shaft, torturing him like he does me. Sometimes, he keeps me on the edge for hours, relentlessly torturing me until I'm so sensitive, all it takes is one touch, and I'm squirting all over him. He loves when he makes me do that.

"Let me taste you," he says.

I slip my hand between my thighs, gasping when I bump my clit. I've barely even started with him, and I'm already soaked and turned on. I touch myself for a minute, whimpering his name. He growls a curse and pulls at the ties as if planning to break free.

"Don't even think about it, Adrian Inácio Kane," I snap.

He narrows his eyes on me.

"It's my turn."

"Then stop touching what's mine, Stella," he growls. "If you make yourself come and it's not on my cock, I'm turning your pretty ass red when I get these fucking ties off."

Oh, he is wicked.

My stomach clenches hard enough to qualify as a mini orgasm.

He notices. "You need to come, *docinho*?" he croons. "Untie me, and I'll lick up all that cream you're making for me before I give you what you need."

"No. I'm not finished yet," I mutter and then lean forward to brush my fingers across his bottom lip.

He growls, his eyes narrowing to slits. And then he runs his tongue across his bottom lip.

I wiggle my way down the bed while he's occupied. His erection bobs in front of my face. I run my hands up his thighs. They are so damn powerful. I never knew a man's legs could be sexy until him.

"You going to suck me off, dimples?" he asks, watching me intently.

"Maybe." I touch him everywhere except where he wants me to go. I kiss his abs and the sexy V, nip at his hipbone, and graze his balls with my fingertips.

He yanks against the ties again, panting. His eyes narrow further, darkening. He curses under his breath, rattling off a string of Portuguese too fast for me to understand. He's been teaching me and the boys to speak the language his mom taught him to love, but I'm still learning. I think he's threatening to spank me again, though.

He's obsessed with my ass and getting his hands on it. And his mouth. And every other part of him. I never knew anal could be so intimate and beautiful. But when he takes me like that, he's always so careful and sweet with me. I love it because it feels so damn good, because he always comes so hard, and because he always cuddles me in the shower afterward. Those little moments where he's taking care of me and loving on me are, hands down, some of the best moments in my life.

I graze his balls again and then the head of his cock.

"Stella," he growls, yanking at the ties again.

I lean forward, taking him as deep as I can.

"Fuck!" he shouts, his hips arching upward, forcing more of him down my throat.

I gag, pulling back to catch my breath.

"Baby, baby," he moans. "Fuck. That hot little mouth."

"I have something to tell you," I murmur and then take him into my mouth again. I suck him hard, wrapping my hand around his shaft to stroke him at the same time. He's so big. It's impossible to fit all of him inside my mouth. I've been trying for five years and still haven't managed it.

"What?" he says, writhing beneath me.

And God, I love seeing that, love knowing he's completely at my mercy. That he's giving up all that control for me. I've seen him throw freaking tires and tree trunks down the beach. He could snap the ties if he really wanted to do it. But he doesn't. He lets me torture him.

I suck him, moving between his cock and his balls until he's on the edge, his balls drawn up, precum dripping from the slit. And then I pull back.

"You're going to be a daddy again," I whisper before plunging down on him.

He roars, his body going taut. His cum spills across my lips and down my throat. I swallow every drop until he's writhing beneath me again, too sensitive for any more. Even then, his erection doesn't abate.

"Untie me," he growls, pulling on the ties again. His eyes are on fire, his expression fierce and feral. He looks like a Titan, larger than life and triumphant.

I quickly scramble up the bed to untie him.

As soon as the ties are undone, I'm on my back beneath him.

"Say it again," he growls.

"You're going to be a daddy again, Adrian," I whisper, smiling. "I'm pregnant."

"*Cristo*," he breathes. His eyes fall closed, a tremor moving through his big body. He stays completely frozen over me for a long moment, processing the news. And then he's inside me, thrusting so deep I cry out his name.

He fucks me hard, pounding into me like he can't stop himself. I claw down his back, writhing beneath him and babbling his name. He wraps his lips around my nipple and then delivers a sharp bite that I feel all the way into my bones.

I come hard, screaming his name as it rips through me without warning. He fucks me through it, not stopping until I'm whimpering beneath him. I whimper again when he pulls out of me, kissing his way down my body. He stops at my belly and nuzzles his face into me. His kisses there are sweet, full of reverence and adoration.

And then he moves on. He pries my legs farther apart, fitting himself between them. His obsidian eyes meet mine, full of wicked intent and sinful promise.

"You don't come again until I decide to let you."

I don't get a chance to respond. He buries his face in my center, yanking my hips up to meet him. He eats me like he hasn't tasted me in years, snarling and growling curses. I grip the sheets in one hand and his hair in the other, hanging on for dear life.

He punishes me with that filthy mouth of his, fucking me with his tongue and then doing the same with my back entrance. He plays with my clit, jiggling it with his tongue and then sucking on it until I'm on the edge of an orgasm, seconds away from falling over the edge.

He pulls back, flipping me over and then pulling my hips up.

"Steady, *docinho*," he croons, catching me when I almost lose my balance. He cradles my belly as if to remind me that I'm pregnant. Warmth flows through me in a powerful wave. Even when he's fucking the air out of my lungs, he's so damn sweet.

As soon as he's sure I'm steady, he slams inside me again. The grunt that leaves his lips is so full of satisfaction, I sob his name.

"Fuck, dimples," he growls, gripping my hip. He fucks me like he means it, pounding into me in deep strikes that leave me sobbing in pleasure. He's relentless, taking what he wants while the bed shakes and rattles beneath us. He runs his hands all over my ass, kneading it, spanking it...worshipping it.

I rock back to meet every hard thrust, helpless to do anything but take it.

He wraps my hair around his fist, pulling my head back to kiss me. Even then, he doesn't let up. He builds me up, higher and higher. Every time I'm right *there*, he changes the pace, moves in some new way. He keeps me on the edge until I'm wrecked beneath him, desperate for relief.

"Please," I whimper, begging for release. My hair is a sweaty mess around his fist, my entire body overheated and overly sensitive. If I don't come soon, I'm going to explode into tiny pieces. "Please let me come. Please, Adrian."

He flips me over onto my back again, looming over me. His cheeks are flushed, his eyes blazing with heat. He's a God above me, fiercely beautiful and beautifully fierce.

"You're carrying my baby," he whispers, awe in his voice. It reflects like stars in his eyes too. He dips his head, raining kisses down on me. *"Eu te amo. Você me completa."*

"Adrian," I sob, tears pooling in my eyes.

"Come for me, dimples," he croons, pressing his thumb to my clit as he makes love to me, all soft and sweet and perfect. "Give it to me."

As soon as he gives me permission, the orgasm blooms in my belly, ripples of ecstasy spiraling outward to consume me. I cry out his name, clawing down his arms as it tears through me. I can't look away from him, can't stop sobbing his name.

He falls with me, roaring wordlessly as he spills inside me again and again.

We pant and writhe and moan, locked together like puzzle pieces made whole again.

It's a long time before I float back to earth, landing gently in his arms. He's wrapped around me like a living blanket, pressing kisses all over my neck and shoulders. One big hand grips my right breast possessively. The other cradles my belly.

"You're really giving me another baby?"

"Yeah," I whisper, a dreamy smile overtaking my face. "I took a test on Tuesday. We're definitely pregnant again."

"I love you," he whispers, punctuating each word with another adoring kiss. "*Cristo*, how I love you, *meu coração*."

I feel his words the same way I feel him. Everywhere. Happy tears leak from the corners of my eyes, bliss flowing through my veins instead of blood. For so long, he was the mystery I wanted to solve. Now, he's the man I get to love unconditionally...and the one who loves me the same way.

I can't think of a better way to spend the rest of my life.

AUTHOR'S NOTE

If you enjoyed Falling Hard, please consider leaving a review! They are so helpful for authors.

Fall in love with Camila and Gray in Ice Breaker, available now!

Ice Breaker

This bossy hockey star is playing for keeps with his publicist's heart.

Gray

As a hockey star, women expect me to be a player.

But dating was never on my agenda until team management made me participate in a Win a Date contest.

My date was a disaster...and now I need a new publicist.

Mine sold the humiliating photos to the press.

Enter Camila Gomes, the curvy Brazilian goddess I can't resist.

She doesn't like athletes and doesn't date clients.

But I'll find a way to prove I'm worth the hassle.

Because there's no way I'm letting this woman get away.

Camila

I knew nothing good would come of agreeing to Kelsey Lane's plea to represent Gray Larsen.

He's hot, bossy, and an athlete...three things I've never handled well.

But when he smiles at me, I go up in flames.

Maybe I should have taken him up on his offer to fire me.

Because the more time I spend around him, the harder it is to tell him no.

Warning

This older hockey player knows exactly what he wants...the heart of his younger, curvy publicist! If you enjoy laugh-out-loud hockey romance, over-the-top declarations, and steamy-sweet romance, you'll love Gray and Camila's story! As always, Nichole Rose titles come complete with a sticky-sweet and guaranteed HEA.

ICE BREAKER IS NOW AVAILABLE.

Instalove Book Club

The Instalove Book Club is now in session!

Get the inside scoop from your favorite instalove authors, meet new authors to love, and snag freebies and bonus content from featured authors every month. The Instalove Book Club newsletter goes out once per week!

Join now to get your hands on bonus scenes and brand-new, exclusive content from our first six featured authors.

Join the Club: http://instaloveinstalovebookclub.com

FOLLOW NICHOLE

Sign-up for Nichole's mailing list at http://author nicholerose.com/newsletter to stay up to date on all new releases and for exclusive ARC giveaways from Nichole Rose.

Want to connect with Nichole and other readers? Join Nichole Rose's Book Beauties on Facebook!

amazon.com/Nichole-Rose/e/B0847QHXPJ

facebook.com/AuthorNicholeRose/

instagram.com/AuthorNicholeRose

twitter.com/AuthNicholeRose

BB bookbub.com/authors/nichole-rose

♪ tiktok.com/@authornicholerose

Also by Nichole Rose

Her Alpha Series

Her Alpha Daddy Next Door

Her Alpha Boss Undercover

Her Alpha's Secret Baby

Her Alpha Protector

Her Date with an Alpha

Her Alpha: The Complete Series

Her Bride Series

His Future Bride

His Stolen Bride

His Secret Bride

His Curvy Bride

His Captive Bride

His Blushing Bride

His Bride: The Complete Series

Claimed Series

Possessing Liberty

Teaching Rowan

Claiming Caroline

Kissing Kennedy

Claimed: The Complete Series

Love on the Clock Series

Adore You

Hold You

Keep You

Protect You

Love on the Clock: The Complete Series

The Billionaires' Club

The Billionaire's Big Bold Weakness

The Billionaire's Big Bold Wish

The Billionaire's Big Bold Woman

The Billionaire's Big Bold Wonder

Playing for Keeps

Cutie Pie

Ice Breaker

Ice Prince

Ice Giant (coming soon)

The Second Generation

A Blushing Bride for Christmas

Silver Spoon MC

The Surgeon

The Heir

The Lawyer

The Prodigy

The Bodyguard (coming soon)

Echoes of Forever

His Christmas Miracle

Taken by the Hitman

Wicked Saint

The Ruined Trilogy

Physical Science

Wrecked

Destination Romance

Romancing the Cowboy

Beach House Beauty

<u>Standalone Titles</u>

A Touch of Summer

Black Velvet

Easy Ride

His Secret Obsession

Dirty Boy

Naughty Little Elf

Devil's Deceit

Dripping Pearls

<u>One Night with You</u>

Falling Hard

Model Behavior

Learning Curve

Angel KissesFind

<u>writing with Loni Ree as Loni Nichole</u>

Dillon's Heart

Razor's Flame

Ryker's Reward (coming soon)

Zane's Rebel (coming soon)

About Nichole Rose

Nichole Rose is a short romance author on the west coast. Her books feature headstrong, sassy women and the alpha males who consume them. From grumpy detectives to country boys with attitude to instalove and over-the-top declarations, nothing is off-limits.

Nichole is sure to have a steamy, sweet story just right for everyone. She fully believes the world is ugly enough without trying to fit falling in love into a one-size-fits-all box. When not writing, Nichole enjoys fine wine, cute shoes, and everything supernatural. She is happily married to the love of her life and is a proud mama to the world's most ridiculous fur-babies.

You can learn more about Nichole and her books at her website .

 amazon.com/Nichole-Rose/e/B0847QHXPJ

facebook.com/AuthorNicholeRose/

instagram.com/AuthorNicholeRose

twitter.com/AuthNicholeRose

bookbub.com/authors/nichole-rose

tiktok.com/@authornicholerose